Translations

Brian Friel was born in Omagh, County Tyrone, in 1929. His plays include *Philadelphia, Here I Come!*, *Translations*, *Faith Healer*, *Making History*, *Dancing at Lughnasa*, *The Home Place* and *Performances*.

'Brian Friel is one of the most accomplished playwrights working in English today. His work is developed around a central poetic vision which has found, and enhanced, a language of theatre to communicate difficult ideas. This language of drama works through wider poetic sensibilities we actually share with the playwright but which we have lost sight of. Brian Friel sharpens our perceptions and makes us able to understand our human condition and the deepening ironies and contradictions of our age. This is his poetic vision.' Michael Etherton, *Contemporary Irish Dramatists* (Macmillan)

by the same author

THE ENEMY WITHIN
PHILADELPHIA, HERE I COME!
THE LOVES OF CASS MAGUIRE
LOVERS
VOLUNTEERS
LIVING QUARTERS
THE FREEDOM OF THE CITY
THREE SISTERS (Chekhov)
ARISTOCRATS
THE COMMUNICATION CORD
MAKING HISTORY
FATHERS AND SONS (after Turgenev)
THE LONDON VERTIGO (after Charles Macklin)
DANCING AT LUGHNASA
WONDERFUL TENNESSEE
MOLLY SWEENEY
GIVE ME YOUR ANSWER, DO
FAITH HEALER
THREE PLAYS AFTER
PERFORMANCES
THE HOME PLACE
UNCLE VANYA (Chekhov)

BRIAN FRIEL: PLAYS ONE
(*Philadelphia, Here I Come!, The Freedom of the City,
Living Quarters, Aristocrats, Faith Healer, Translations*)

BRIAN FRIEL: PLAYS TWO
(*Dancing at Lughnasa, Fathers and Sons, Making History,
Wonderful Tennessee, Molly Sweeney*)

also available

FABER CRITICAL GUIDE: BRIAN FRIEL
(*Philadelphia, Here I Come!, Translations,
Making History, Dancing at Lughnasa*)

ABOUT FRIEL: THE PLAYWRIGHT AND THE WORK

BRIAN FRIEL

Translations

faber and faber

First published in 1981
by Faber and Faber Limited
Bloomsbury House, 74-77 Great Russell Street,
London WC1B 3DA

Reset in 200 0

Photoset by Parker Typesetting Service, Leicester
Printed and bound by CPI Group (UK) Ltd, Croydon, CR0 4YY

All right reserved

© Brian Friel, 1981

All rights in this play are reserved by the Proprietor
Applications for professional rights should be
addressed to The Agency (London) Ltd,
24 Pottery Lane, Holland Park, London W11 4LZ
The amateur rights for this play are held by Samuel French
Amateur applications for permissions to perform this play must
be made in advance, before rehearsals begin, to
Samuel French Ltd., 52 Fitzroy Street, London W1P 6JR.
No performance may be given unless a licence has first been obtained.

*This book is sold subject to the condition that it shall not, by way of trade
or otherwise, be lent, resold, hired out or otherwise circulated without the
publisher's prior consent in any form of binding or cover other than that
in which it is being published and without a similar condition including
this condition being imposed on the subsequent purchaser.*

A CIP record for this book
is available from the British Library

ISBN 978-0-571-11742-0

for
Stephen Rea

The publisher acknowledges with thanks the financial
assistance of the Arts Council of Northern Ireland
in the publication of this volume.

Translations was first presented by Field Day Theatre Company in the Guildhall, Derry, on Tuesday, 23 September 1980 with the following cast:

Manus Mick Lally
Sarah Ann Hasson
Jimmy Jack Roy Hanlon
Maire Nuala Hayes
Doalty Liam Neeson
Bridget Brenda Scallon
Hugh Ray McAnally
Owen Stephen Rea
Captain Lancey David Heap
Lieutenant Yolland Shaun Scott

Directed by Art O Briain
Designed by Consolata Boyle
Assisted by Magdalena Rubalcava and Mary Friel
Lighting by Rupert Murray

Field Day Theatre Company was formed by Brian Friel and Stephen Rea. *Translations* was their first production.

The action takes place in a hedge-school in the townland of Baile Beag/Ballybeg, an Irish-speaking community in County Donegal.

ACT ONE   An afternoon in late August 1833.
ACT TWO   A few days later.
ACT THREE The evening of the following day.

(For the convenience of readers and performers unfamiliar with the language, roman letters have been used for the Greek words and quotations in the text. The originals, together with the Latin and literal translations, appear in the Appendix.)

Act One

The hedge-school is held in a disused barn or hay-shed or byre. Along the back wall are the remains of five or six stalls – wooden posts and chains – where cows were once milked and bedded. A double door left, large enough to allow a cart to enter. A window right. A wooden stairway without a banister leads to the upstairs living-quarters (off) of the schoolmaster and his son. Around the room are broken and forgotten implements: a cart-wheel, some lobster-pots, farming tools, a battle of hay, a churn, etc. There are also the stools and bench-seats which the pupils use and a table and chair for the master. At the door a pail of water and a soiled towel. The room is comfortless and dusty and functional – there is no trace of a woman's hand.

When the play opens, Manus is teaching Sarah to speak. He kneels beside her. She is sitting on a low stool, her head down, very tense, clutching a slate on her knees. He is coaxing her gently and firmly and – as with everything he does – with a kind of zeal.

Manus is in his late twenties/early thirties; the master's older son. He is pale-faced, lightly built, intense, and works as an unpaid assistant – a monitor – to his father. His clothes are shabby; and when he moves we see that he is lame.

Sarah's speech defect is so bad that all her life she has been considered locally to be dumb and she has accepted this: when she wishes to communicate, she grunts and makes unintelligible nasal sounds. She has a waiflike appearance and could be any age from seventeen to thirty-five.

Jimmy Jack Cassie – known as the Infant Prodigy – sits by himself, contentedly reading Homer in Greek and smiling to himself. He is a bachelor in his sixties, lives alone, and comes to these evening classes partly for the company and partly for the intellectual stimulation. He is fluent in Latin and Greek but is in no way pedantic – to him it is perfectly normal to speak these tongues. He never washes. His clothes – heavy top coat, hat, mittens, which he wears now – are filthy and he lives in them summer and winter, day and night. He now reads in a quiet voice and smiles in profound satisfaction. For Jimmy the world of the gods and the ancient myths is as real and as immediate as everyday life in the townland of Baile Beag.

Manus holds Sarah's hands in his and he articulates slowly and distinctly into her face.

Manus We're doing very well. And we're going to try it once more – just once more. Now – relax and breathe in ... deep ... and out ... in ... and out ...

Sarah shakes her head vigorously and stubbornly.

Come on, Sarah. This is our secret.

Again vigorous and stubborn shaking of Sarah's head.

Nobody's listening. Nobody hears you.

Jimmy '*Ton d'emeibet epeita thea glaukopis Athene ...*'

Manus Get your tongue and your lips working. 'My name – ' Come on. One more try. 'My name is – ' Good girl.

Sarah My ...

Manus Great. 'My name – '

Sarah My ... my ...

Manus Raise your head. Shout it out. Nobody's listening.

Jimmy '... *alla hekelos estai en Atreidao domois ...*'

Manus Jimmy, please! Once more – just once more – 'My name – ' Good girl. Come on now. Head up. Mouth open.

Sarah My...

Manus Good.

Sarah My...

Manus Great.

Sarah My name...

Manus Yes?

Sarah My name is...

Manus Yes?

Sarah pauses. Then in a rush:

Sarah My name is Sarah.

Manus Marvellous! Bloody marvellous!

Manus hugs Sarah. She smiles in shy, embarrassed pleasure.

Did you hear that, Jimmy? – 'My name is Sarah' – clear as a bell. (*to Sarah*) The Infant Prodigy doesn't know what we're at.

Sarah laughs at this. Manus hugs her again and stands up.

Now we're really started! Nothing'll stop us now! Nothing in the wide world!

Jimmy, chuckling at his text, comes over to them.

Jimmy Listen to this, Manus.

Manus Soon you'll be telling me all the secrets that have been in that head of yours all these years.
Certainly, James – what is it?
(*to Sarah*) Maybe you'd set out the stools?

Manus runs up the stairs.

Jimmy Wait till you hear this, Manus.

Manus Go ahead! I'll be straight down.

Jimmy '*Hos ara min phamene rabdo epemassat Athene –*' 'After Athene had said this, she touched Ulysses with her wand. She withered the fair skin of his supple limbs and destroyed the flaxen hair from off his head and about his limbs she put the skin of an old man …'! The divil! The divil!

Manus has emerged again with a bowl of milk and a piece of bread.

And wait till you hear! She's not finished with him yet!

As Manus descends the stairs he toasts Sarah with his bowl.

'*Knuzosen de oi osse –*' 'She dimmed his two eyes that were so beautiful and clothed him in a vile ragged cloak begrimed with filthy smoke …'! Do you see! Smoke! Smoke! D'you see! Sure look at what the same turf-smoke has done to myself! (*He rapidly removes his hat to display his bald head.*) Would you call that flaxen hair?

Manus Of course I would.

Jimmy 'And about him she cast the great skin of a filthy hind, stripped of the hair, and into his hand she thrust a staff and a wallet'! Ha-ha-ha! Athene did that to Ulysses! Made him into a tramp! Isn't she the tight one?

Manus You couldn't watch her, Jimmy.

Jimmy You know what they call her?

Manus '*Glaukopis Athene.*'

Jimmy That's it! The flashing-eyed Athene! By God,

Manus, sir, if you had a woman like that about the house, it's not stripping a turf-bank you'd be thinking about – eh?

Manus She was a goddess, Jimmy.

Jimmy Better still. Sure isn't our own Grania a class of a goddess and –

Manus Who?

Jimmy Grania – Grania – Diarmuid's Grania.

Manus Ah.

Jimmy And sure she can't get her fill of men.

Manus Jimmy, you're impossible.

Jimmy I was just thinking to myself last night: if you had the choosing between Athene and Artemis and Helen of Troy – all three of them Zeus's girls – imagine three powerful-looking daughters like that all in the one parish of Athens! – now, if you had the picking between them, which would you take?

Manus (*to Sarah*) Which should I take, Sarah?

Jimmy No harm to Helen; and no harm to Artemis; and indeed no harm to our own Grania, Manus. But I think I've no choice but to go bull-straight for Athene. By God, sir, them flashing eyes would fair keep a man jigged up constant!

Suddenly and momentarily, as if in spasm, Jimmy stands to attention and salutes, his face raised in pained ecstasy.

Manus laughs. So does Sarah. Jimmy goes back to his seat, and his reading.

Manus You're a dangerous bloody man, Jimmy Jack.

Jimmy 'Flashing-eyed'! Hah! Sure Homer knows it all, boy. Homer knows it all.

Manus goes to the window and looks out.

Manus Where the hell has he got to?

Sarah goes to Manus and touches his elbow. She mimes rocking a baby.

Yes, I know he's at the christening; but it doesn't take them all day to put a name on a baby, does it?

Sarah mimes pouring drinks and tossing them back quickly.

You may be sure. Which pub?

Sarah indicates.

Gracie's?

No. Further away.

Con Connie Tim's?

No. To the right of there.

Anna na mBreag's?

Yes. That's it.

Great. She'll fill him up. I suppose I may take the class then.

Manus begins to distribute some books, slates and chalk, texts etc. beside the seats.
Sarah goes over to the straw and produces a bunch of flowers she has hidden there.
During this:

Jimmy '*Autar o ek limenos prosebe* –' 'But Ulysses went forth from the harbour and through the woodland to the place where Athene had shown him he could find the good swineherd who – '*o oi biotoio malista kedeto*' – what's that, Manus?

Manus 'Who cared most for his substance'.

Jimmy That's it! 'The good swineherd who cared most for his substance above all the slaves that Ulysses possessed ...'

Sarah presents the flowers to Manus.

Manus Those are lovely, Sarah.

But Sarah has fled in embarrassment to her seat and has her head buried in a book. Manus goes to her.

Flow-ers.

Pause. Sarah does not look up.

Say the word: flow-ers. Come on – flow-ers.

Sarah Flowers.

Manus You see? – you're off!

Manus leans down and kisses the top of Sarah's head.

And they're beautiful flowers. Thank you.

Maire *enters, a strong-minded, strong-bodied woman in her twenties with a head of curly hair. She is carrying a small can of milk.*

Maire Is this all's here? Is there no school this evening?

Manus If my father's not back, I'll take it.

Manus stands awkwardly, having been caught kissing Sarah and with the flowers almost formally at his chest.

Maire Well now, isn't that a pretty sight. There's your milk. How's Sarah?

Sarah grunts a reply.

Manus I saw you out at the hay.

Maire ignores this and goes to Jimmy.

Maire And how's Jimmy Jack Cassie?

Jimmy Sit down beside me, Maire.

Maire Would I be safe?

Jimmy No safer man in Donegal.

Maire flops on a stool beside Jimmy.

Maire Ooooh. The best harvest in living memory, they say; but I don't want to see another like it. (*Showing Jimmy her hands.*) Look at the blisters.

Jimmy *Esne fatigata?*

Maire *Sum fatigatissima.*

Jimmy *Bene! Optime!*

Maire That's the height of my Latin. Fit me better if I had even that much English.

Jimmy English? I thought you had some English?

Maire Three words. Wait – there was a spake I used to have off by heart. What's this it was?

Her accent is strange because she is speaking a foreign language and because she does not understand what she is saying.

'In Norfolk we besport ourselves around the maypoll.' What about that!

Manus Maypole.

Again Maire ignores Manus.

Maire God have mercy on my Aunt Mary – she taught me that when I was about four, whatever it means. Do you know what it means, Jimmy?

Jimmy Sure you know I have only Irish like yourself.

Maire And Latin. And Greek.

Jimmy I'm telling you a lie: I know one English word.

Maire What?

Jimmy Bo-som.

Maire What's a bo-som?

Jimmy You know – (*He illustrates with his hands.*) – bo-som – bo-som – you know – Diana, the huntress, she has two powerful bosom.

Maire You may be sure that's the one English word you would know. (*Rises.*) Is there a drop of water about?

Manus gives Maire his bowl of milk.

Manus I'm sorry I couldn't get up last night.

Maire Doesn't matter.

Manus Biddy Hanna sent for me to write a letter to her sister in Nova Scotia. All the gossip of the parish. 'I brought the cow to the bull three times last week but no good. There's nothing for it now but Big Ned Frank.'

Maire (*drinking*) That's better.

Manus And she got so engrossed in it that she forgot who she was dictating to: 'The aul drunken schoolmaster and that lame son of his are still footering about in the hedge-school, wasting people's good time and money.'

Maire has to laugh at this.

Maire She did not!

Manus And me taking it all down. 'Thank God one of them new national schools is being built above at Poll na gCaorach.' It was after midnight by the time I got back.

Maire Great to be a busy man.

Maire moves away. Manus follows.

Manus I could hear music on my way past but I thought it was too late to call.

Maire (*to Sarah*) Wasn't your father in great voice last night?

Sarah nods and smiles.

It must have been near three o'clock by the time you got home?

Sarah holds up four fingers.

Was it four? No wonder we're in pieces.

Manus I can give you a hand at the hay tomorrow.

Maire That's the name of a hornpipe, isn't it? – 'The Scholar in the Hayfield' – or is it a reel?

Manus If the day's good.

Maire Suit yourself. The English soldiers below in the tents, them sapper fellows, they're coming up to give us a hand. I don't know a word they're saying, nor they me; but sure that doesn't matter, does it?

Manus What the hell are you so crabbed about?!

> **Doalty** *and* **Bridget** *enter noisily. Both are in their twenties.*
> *Doalty is brandishing a surveyor's pole. He is an open-minded, open-hearted, generous and slightly thick young man.*
> *Bridget is a plump, fresh young girl, ready to laugh, vain, and with a countrywoman's instinctive cunning.*
> *Doalty enters doing his imitation of the master.*

Doalty Vesperal salutations to you all.

Bridget He's coming down past Carraig na Ri and he's as full as a pig!

Doalty *Ignari, stulti, rustici* – pot-boys and peasant whelps – semi-literates and illegitimates.

Bridget He's been on the batter since this morning; he sent the wee ones home at eleven o'clock.

Doalty Three questions. Question A – Am I drunk? Question B – Am I sober? (*into Maire's face*) *Responde – responde!*

Bridget Question C, Master – When were you last sober?

Maire What's the weapon, Doalty?

Bridget I warned him. He'll be arrested one of these days.

Doalty Up in the bog with Bridget and her aul fella, and the Red Coats were just across at the foot of Cnoc na Mona, dragging them aul chains and peeping through that big machine they lug about everywhere with them – you know the name of it, Manus?

Maire Theodolite.

Bridget How do you know?

Maire They leave it in our byre at night sometimes if it's raining.

Jimmy Theodolite – what's the etymology of that word, Manus?

Manus No idea.

Bridget Get on with the story.

Jimmy *Theo – theos* – something to do with a god. Maybe *thea* – a goddess! What shape's the yoke?

Doalty 'Shape!' Will you shut up, you aul eejit you! Anyway, every time they'd stick one of these poles into the ground and move across the bog, I'd creep up and shift it twenty or thirty paces to the side.

Bridget God!

Doalty Then they'd come back and stare at it and look at their calculations and stare at it again and scratch their heads. And Cripes, d'you know what they ended up doing?

Bridget Wait till you hear!

Doalty They took the bloody machine apart! (*And immediately he speaks in gibberish – an imitation of two very agitated and confused sappers in rapid conversation.*)

Bridget That's the image of them!

Maire You must be proud of yourself, Doalty.

Doalty What d'you mean?

Maire That was a very clever piece of work.

Manus It was a gesture.

Maire What sort of a gesture?

Manus Just to indicate ... a presence.

Maire Hah!

Bridget I'm telling you – you'll be arrested.

When Doalty is embarrassed – or pleased – he reacts physically. He now grabs Bridget around the waist.

Doalty What d'you make of that for an implement, Bridget? Wouldn't that make a great aul shaft for your churn?

Bridget Let go of me, you dirty brute! I've a headline to do before Big Hughie comes.

Manus I don't think we'll wait for him. Let's get started.

Slowly, reluctantly they begin to move to their seats and

specific tasks. Doalty goes to the bucket of water at the door and washes his hands. Bridget sets up a hand-mirror and combs her hair.

Bridget Nellie Ruadh's baby was to be christened this morning. Did any of yous hear what she called it? Did you, Sarah?

Sarah grunts: No.

Did you, Maire?

Maire No.

Bridget Our Seamus says she was threatening she was going to call it after its father.

Doalty Who's the father?

Bridget That's the point, you donkey you!

Doalty Ah.

Bridget So there's a lot of uneasy bucks about Baile Beag this day.

Doalty She told me last Sunday she was going to call it Jimmy.

Bridget You're a liar, Doalty.

Doalty Would I tell you a lie? Hi, Jimmy, Nellie Ruadh's aul fella's looking for you.

Jimmy For me?

Maire Come on, Doalty.

Doalty Someone told him ...

Maire Doalty!

Doalty He heard you know the first book of the Satires of Horace off by heart ...

Jimmy That's true.

Doalty ... and he wants you to recite it for him.

Jimmy I'll do that for him certainly, certainly.

Doalty He's busting to hear it.

Jimmy fumbles in his pockets.

Jimmy I came across this last night – this'll interest you – in Book Two of Virgil's *Georgics*.

Doalty Be God, that's my territory all right.

Bridget You clown you! (*to Sarah*) Hold this for me, would you? (*her mirror*)

Jimmy Listen to this, Manus. '*Nigra fere et presso pinguis sub vomere terra ...*'

Doalty Steady on now – easy, boys, easy – don't rush me, boys – (*He mimes great concentration.*)

Jimmy Manus?

Manus 'Land that is black and rich beneath the pressure of the plough ...'

Doalty Give *me* a chance!

Jimmy 'And with *cui putre* – with crumbly soil – is in the main best for corn.' There you are.

Doalty There you are.

Jimmy 'From no other land will you see more wagons wending homeward behind slow bullocks.' Virgil! There!

Doalty 'Slow bullocks'!

Jimmy Isn't that what I'm always telling you? Black soil for corn. *That's* what you should have in that upper field of yours – corn, not spuds.

Doalty Would you listen to that fella! Too lazy be Jasus to wash himself and he's lecturing me on agriculture! Would you go and take a running race at yourself, Jimmy Jack Cassie! (*Grabs Sarah.*) Come away out of this with me, Sarah, and we'll plant some corn together.

Manus All right – all right. Let's settle down and get some work done. I know Sean Beag isn't coming – he's at the salmon. What about the Donnelly twins? (*to Doalty*) Are the Donnelly twins not coming any more?

Doalty shrugs and turns away.

Did you ask them?

Doalty Haven't seen them. Not about these days.

Doalty begins whistling through his teeth. Suddenly the atmosphere is silent and alert.

Manus Aren't they at home?

Doalty No.

Manus Where are they then?

Doalty How would I know?

Bridget Our Seamus says two of the soldiers' horses were found last night at the foot of the cliffs at Machaire Buide and ... (*She stops suddenly and begins writing with chalk on her slate.*) D'you hear the whistles of this aul slate? Sure nobody could write on an aul slippery thing like that.

Manus What headline did my father set you?

Bridget 'It's easier to stamp out learning than to recall it.'

Jimmy Book Three, the *Agricola* of Tacitus.

Bridget God but you're a dose.

Manus Can you do it?

Bridget There. Is it bad? Will he ate me?

Manus It's very good. Keep your elbow in closer to your side. Doalty?

Doalty I'm at the seven-times table. I'm perfect, skipper.

Manus moves to Sarah.

Manus Do you understand those sums?

Sarah nods: Yes. Manus leans down to her ear.

My name is Sarah.

Manus goes to Maire. While he is talking to her the others swap books, talk quietly, etc.

Can I help you? What are you at?

Maire Map of America. (*Pause.*) The passage money came last Friday.

Manus You never told me that.

Maire Because I haven't seen you since, have I?

Manus You don't want to go. You said that yourself.

Maire There's ten below me to be raised and no man in the house. What do you suggest?

Manus Do you want to go?

Maire Did you apply for that job in the new national school?

Manus No.

Maire You said you would.

Manus I said I might.

Maire When it opens, this is finished: nobody's going to pay to go to a hedge-school.

Manus I know that and I ...

He breaks off because he sees Sarah, obviously listening, at his shoulder. She moves away again.

I was thinking that maybe I could ...

Maire It's £56 a year you're throwing away.

Manus I can't apply for it.

Maire You *promised* me you would.

Manus My father has applied for it.

Maire He has not!

Manus Day before yesterday.

Maire For God's sake, sure you know he'd never –

Manus I couldn't – I can't go in against him.

Maire looks at him for a second. Then:

Maire Suit yourself. (*to Bridget*) I saw your Seamus heading off to the Port fair early this morning.

Bridget And wait till you hear this – I forgot to tell you this. He said that as soon as he crossed over the gap at Cnoc na Mona – just beyond where the soldiers are making the maps – the sweet smell was everywhere.

Doalty You never told me that.

Bridget It went out of my head.

Doalty He saw the crops in Port?

Bridget Some.

Manus How did the tops look?

Bridget Fine – I think.

Doalty In flower?

Bridget I don't know. I think so. He didn't say.

Manus Just the sweet smell – that's all?

Bridget They say that's the way it snakes in, don't they? First the smell; and then one morning the stalks are all black and limp.

Doalty Are you stupid? It's the rotting stalks makes the sweet smell for God's sake. That's what the smell is – rotting stalks.

Maire Sweet smell! Sweet smell! Every year at this time somebody comes back with stories of the sweet smell. Sweet God, did the potatoes ever fail in Baile Beag? Well, did they ever – ever? Never! There was never blight here. Never. Never. But we're always sniffing about for it, aren't we? – looking for disaster. The rents are going to go up again – the harvest's going to be lost – the herring have gone away for ever – there's going to be evictions. Honest to God, some of you people aren't happy unless you're miserable and you'll not be content until you're dead!

Doalty Bloody right, Maire. And sure St. Colmcille prophesied there'd never be blight here. He said:

The spuds will bloom in Baile Beag
Till rabbits grow an extra lug.

And sure that'll never be. So we're all right.
Seven threes are twenty-one; seven fours are twenty-eight; seven fives are forty-nine – Hi, Jimmy, do you fancy my chances as boss of the new national school?

Jimmy What's that? – what's that?

Doalty Agh, g'way back home to Greece, son.

Maire You ought to apply, Doalty.

Doalty D'you think so? Cripes, maybe I will. Hah!

Bridget Did you know that you start at the age of six and you have to stick at it until you're twelve at least – no matter how smart you are or how much you know.

Doalty Who told you that yarn?

Bridget And every child from every house has to go all day, every day, summer or winter. That's the law.

Doalty I'll tell you something – nobody's going to go near them – they're not going to take on – law or no law.

Bridget And everything's free in them. You pay for nothing except the books you use; that's what our Seamus says.

Doalty 'Our Seamus'. Sure your Seamus wouldn't pay anyway. She's making this all up.

Bridget Isn't that right, Manus?

Manus I think so.

Bridget And from the very first day you go, you'll not hear one word of Irish spoken. You'll be taught to speak English and every subject will be taught through English and everyone'll end up as cute as the Buncrana people.

Sarah suddenly grunts and mimes a warning that the master is coming. The atmosphere changes. Sudden business. Heads down.

Doalty He's here, boys. Cripes, he'll make yella meal out of me for those bloody tables.

Bridget Have you any extra chalk, Manus?

Maire And the atlas for me.

Doalty goes to Maire who is sitting on a stool at the back.

Doalty Swap you seats.

Maire Why?

Doalty There's an empty one beside the Infant Prodigy.

Maire I'm fine here.

Doalty Please, Maire. I want to jouk in the back here.

Maire rises.

God love you. (*aloud*) Anyone got a bloody table-book? Cripes, I'm wrecked.

Sarah gives him one.

God, I'm dying about you.

In his haste to get to the back seat Doalty bumps into Bridget who is kneeling on the floor and writing laboriously on a slate resting on top of a bench-seat.

Bridget Watch where you're going, Doalty!

Doalty gooses Bridget. She squeals.
   Now the quiet hum of work: Jimmy reading Homer in a low voice; Bridget copying her headline; Maire studying the atlas; Doalty, his eyes shut tight, mouthing his tables; Sarah doing sums.
   After a few seconds:

Bridget Is this 'g' right, Manus? How do you put a tail on it?

Doalty Will you shut up! I can't concentrate!

A few more seconds of work. Then Doalty opens his eyes and looks around.

False alarm, boys. The bugger's not coming at all. Sure the bugger's hardly fit to walk.

And immediately Hugh enters. A large man, with residual dignity, shabbily dressed, carrying a stick. He has, as always, a large quantity of drink taken, but he is by no means drunk. He is in his early sixties.

Hugh *Adsum*, Doalty, *adsum*. Perhaps not in *sobrietate perfecta* but adequately *sobrius* to overhear your quip. Vesperal salutations to you all.

Various responses.

Jimmy *Ave*, Hugh.

Hugh James.

He removes his hat and coat and hands them and his stick to Manus, as if to a footman.

Apologies for my late arrival: we were celebrating the baptism of Nellie Ruadh's baby.

Bridget (*innocently*) What name did she put on it, Master?

Hugh Was it Eamon? Yes, it was Eamon.

Bridget Eamon Donal from Tor! Cripes!

Hugh And after the *caerimonia nominationis* – Maire?

Maire The ritual of naming.

Hugh Indeed – we then had a few libations to mark the occasion. Altogether very pleasant. The derivation of the word 'baptise'? – where are my Greek scholars? Doalty?

Doalty Would it be – ah – ah –

Hugh Too slow. James?

Jimmy '*Baptizein*' – to dip or immerse.

Hugh Indeed – our friend Pliny Minor speaks of the '*baptisterium*' – the cold bath.

Doalty Master.

Hugh Doalty?

Doalty I suppose you could talk then about baptising a sheep at sheep-dipping, could you?

Laughter. Comments.

Hugh Indeed – the precedent is there – the day you were appropriately named Doalty – seven nines?

Doalty What's that, Master?

Hugh Seven times nine?

Doalty Seven nines – seven nines – seven times nine – seven times nine are – Cripes, it's on the tip of my tongue, Master – I knew it for sure this morning – funny that's the only one that foxes me –

Bridget (*prompt*) Sixty-three.

Doalty What's wrong with me: sure seven nines are fifty-three, Master.

Hugh Sophocles from Colonus would agree with Doalty Dan Doalty from Tulach Alainn: 'To know nothing is the sweetest life.' Where's Sean Beag?

Manus He's at the salmon.

Hugh And Nora Dan?

Maire She says she's not coming back any more.

Hugh Ah. Nora Dan can now write her name – Nora Dan's education is complete. And the Donnelly twins?

Brief pause. Then:

Bridget They're probably at the turf. (*She goes to Hugh.*) There's the one-and-eight I owe you for last quarter's arithmetic and there's my one-and-six for this quarter's writing.

Hugh *Gratias tibi ago.* (*He sits at his table.*)
Before we commence our *studia* I have three items of
information to impart to you – (*to Manus*) a bowl of tea,
strong tea, black –

Manus leaves.

Item A: on my perambulations today – Bridget? Too slow.
Maire?

Maire *Perambulare* – to walk about.

Hugh Indeed – I encountered Captain Lancey of the Royal
Engineers who is engaged in the ordnance survey of this
area. He tells me that in the past few days two of his
horses have strayed and some of his equipment seems to
be mislaid. I expressed my regret and suggested he address
you himself on these matters. He then explained that he
does not speak Irish. Latin? I asked. None. Greek? Not a
syllable. He speaks – on his own admission – only English;
and to his credit he seemed suitably verecund – James?

James *Verecundus* – humble.

Hugh Indeed – he voiced some surprise that we did not
speak his language. I explained that a few of us did, on
occasion – outside the parish of course – and then usually
for the purposes of commerce, a use to which his tongue
seemed particularly suited – (*shouts*) and a slice of soda
bread – and I went on to propose that our own culture and
the classical tongues made a happier conjugation – Doalty?

Doalty *Conjugo* – I join together.

*Doalty is so pleased with himself that he prods and
winks at Bridget.*

Hugh Indeed – English, I suggested, couldn't really
express us. And again to his credit he acquiesced to my
logic. Acquiesced – Maire?

Maire turns away impatiently. Hugh is unaware of the gesture.

Too slow. Bridget?

Bridget *Acquiesco.*

Hugh *Procede.*

Bridget *Acquiesco, acquiescere, acquievi, acquietum.*

Hugh Indeed – and Item B ...

Maire Master.

Hugh Yes?

Maire gets to her feet uneasily but determinedly. Pause.

Well, girl?

Maire We should all be learning to speak English. That's what my mother says. That's what I say. That's what Dan O'Connell said last month in Ennis. He said the sooner we all learn to speak English the better.

Suddenly several speak together.

Jimmy What's she saying? What? What?

Doalty It's Irish he uses when he's travelling around scrounging votes.

Bridget And sleeping with married women. Sure no woman's safe from that fella.

Jimmy Who-who-who? Who's this? Who's this?

Hugh *Silentium!* (*Pause.*) Who is she talking about?

Maire I'm talking about Daniel O'Connell.

Hugh Does she mean that little Kerry politician?

Maire I'm talking about the Liberator, Master, as you well know. And what he said was this: 'The old language is a barrier to modern progress.' He said that last month. And he's right. I don't want Greek. I don't want Latin. I want English.

Manus reappears on the platform above.

I want to be able to speak English because I'm going to America as soon as the harvest's all saved.

Maire remains standing. Hugh puts his hand into his pocket and produces a flask of whisky. He removes the cap, pours a drink into it, tosses it back, replaces the cap, puts the flask back into his pocket. Then:

Hugh We have been diverted – *diverto* – *divertere* – Where were we?

Doalty Three items of information, Master. You're at Item B.

Hugh Indeed – Item B – Item B – yes – On my way to the christening this morning I chanced to meet Mr George Alexander, Justice of the Peace. We discussed the new national school. Mr Alexander invited me to take charge of it when it opens. I thanked him and explained that I could do that only if I were free to run it as I have run this hedge-school for the past thirty-five years – filling what our friend Euripides calls the '*aplestos pithos*' – James?

Jimmy 'The cask that cannot be filled'.

Hugh Indeed – and Mr Alexander retorted courteously and emphatically that he hopes that is how it will be run.

Maire now sits.

Indeed. I have had a strenuous day and I am weary of you all. (*He rises.*) Manus will take care of you.

Hugh goes towards the steps.

Owen enters. Owen is the younger son, a handsome, attractive young man in his twenties. He is dressed smartly – a city man. His manner is easy and charming: everything he does is invested with consideration and enthusiasm. He now stands framed in the doorway, a travelling bag across his shoulder.

Owen Could anybody tell me is this where Hugh Mor O'Donnell holds his hedge-school?

Doalty It's Owen – Owen Hugh! Look boys – it's Owen Hugh!

Owen enters. As he crosses the room he touches and has a word for each person.

Owen Doalty! (*playful punch*) How are you, boy? *Jacobe, quid agis?* Are you well?

Jimmy Fine. Fine.

Owen And Bridget! Give us a kiss. Aaaaaah!

Bridget You're welcome, Owen.

Owen It's not – ? Yes, it *is* Maire Chatach! God! A young woman!

Maire How are you, Owen?

Owen is now in front of Hugh. He puts his two hands on his father's shoulders.

Owen And how's the old man himself?

Hugh Fair – fair.

Owen Fair? For God's sake you never looked better! Come here to me. (*He embraces Hugh warmly and genuinely.*) Great to see you, Father. Great to be back.

Hugh's eyes are moist – partly joy, partly the drink.

Hugh I – I'm – I'm – pay no attention to –

Owen Come on – come on – come on – (*He gives Hugh his handkerchief.*) Do you know what you and I are going to do tonight? We are going to go up to Anna na mBreag's...

Doalty Not there, Owen.

Owen Why not?

Doalty Her poteen's worse than ever.

Bridget They say she puts frogs in it!

Owen All the better. (*to Hugh.*) And you and I are going to get footless drunk. That's arranged.

Owen sees Manus coming down the steps with tea and soda bread. They meet at the bottom.

And Manus!

Manus You're welcome, Owen.

Owen I know I am. And it's great to be here. (*He turns round, arms outstretched.*) I can't believe it. I come back after six years and everything's just as it was! Nothing's changed! Not a thing! (*Sniffs.*) Even that smell – that's the same smell this place always had. What is it anyway? Is it the straw?

Doalty Jimmy Jack's feet.

General laughter. It opens little pockets of conversation round the room.

Owen And Doalty Dan Doalty hasn't changed either!

Doalty Bloody right, Owen.

Owen Jimmy, are you well?

Jimmy Dodging about.

Owen Any word of the big day?

This is greeted with 'ohs' and 'ahs'.

Time enough, Jimmy. Homer's easier to live with, isn't he?

Maire We heard stories that you own ten big shops in Dublin – is it true?

Owen Only nine.

Bridget And you've twelve horses and six servants.

Owen Yes – that's true. God Almighty, would you listen to them – taking a hand at me!

Manus When did you arrive?

Owen We left Dublin yesterday morning, spent last night in Omagh and got here half an hour ago.

Manus You're hungry then.

Hugh Indeed – get him food – get him a drink.

Owen Not now, thanks; later. Listen – am I interrupting you all?

Hugh By no means. We're finished for the day.

Owen Wonderful. I'll tell you why. Two friends of mine are waiting outside the door. They'd like to meet you and I'd like you to meet them. May I bring them in?

Hugh Certainly. You'll all eat and have ...

Owen Not just yet, Father. You've seen the sappers working in this area for the past fortnight, haven't you? Well, the older man is Captain Lancey ...

Hugh I've met Captain Lancey.

Owen Great. He's the cartographer in charge of this whole area. Cartographer – James?

Owen begins to play this game – his father's game – partly to involve his classroom audience, partly to show he has not forgotten it, and indeed partly because he enjoys it.

Jimmy A maker of maps.

Owen Indeed – and the younger man that I travelled with from Dublin, his name is Lieutenant Yolland and he is attached to the toponymic department – Father? – *responde – responde*!

Hugh He gives names to places.

Owen Indeed – although he is in fact an orthographer – Doalty? – too slow – Manus?

Manus The correct spelling of those names.

Owen Indeed – indeed!

Owen laughs and claps his hands. Some of the others join in.

Beautiful! Beautiful! Honest to God, it's such a delight to be back here with you all again – '*civilised*' people. Anyhow – may I bring them in?

Hugh Your friends are our friends.

Owen I'll be straight back.

There is general talk as Owen goes towards the door. He stops beside Sarah.

That's a new face. Who are you?

A very brief hesitation. Then:

Sarah My name is Sarah.

Owen Sarah who?

Sarah Sarah John Sally.

Owen Of course! From Bun na hAbhann! I'm Owen – Owen Hugh Mor. From Baile Beag. Good to see you.

During this Owen–Sarah exchange:

Hugh Come on now. Let's tidy this place up. (*He rubs the top of his table with his sleeve.*) Move, Doalty – lift those books off the floor.

Doalty Right, Master; certainly, Master; I'm doing my best, Master.

Owen stops at the door.

Owen One small thing, Father.

Hugh *Silentium*!

Owen I'm on their pay-roll.

Sarah, very elated at her success, is beside Manus.

Sarah I said it, Manus!

Manus ignores Sarah. He is much more interested in Owen now.

Manus You haven't enlisted, have you?!

Sarah moves away.

Owen Me a soldier? I'm employed as a part-time, underpaid, civilian interpreter. My job is to translate the quaint, archaic tongue you people persist in speaking into the King's good English. (*He goes out.*)

Hugh Move – move – move! Put some order on things! Come on, Sarah – hide that bucket. Whose are these slates? Somebody take these dishes away. *Festinate! Festinate!* (*He pours another drink.*)

Manus goes to Maire who is busy tidying.

Manus You didn't tell me you were definitely leaving.

Maire Not now.

Hugh Good girl, Bridget. That's the style.

Manus You might at least have told me.

Hugh Are these your books, James?

Jimmy Thank you.

Manus Fine! Fine! Go ahead! Go ahead!

Maire You talk to me about getting married – with neither a roof over your head nor a sod of ground under your foot. I suggest you go for the new school; but no – 'My father's in for that.' Well now he's got it and now this is finished and now you've nothing.

Manus I can always ...

Maire What? Teach classics to the cows? Agh –

Maire moves away from Manus.
Owen enters with Lancey, and Yolland. Captain Lancey is middle-aged; a small, crisp officer, expert in his field as cartographer but uneasy with people – especially civilians, especially these foreign civilians. His skill is with deeds, not words.
Lieutenant Yolland is in his late twenties/early thirties. He is tall and thin and gangling, blond hair, a shy, awkward manner. A soldier by accident.

Owen Here we are. Captain Lancey – my father.

Lancey Good evening.

Hugh becomes expansive, almost courtly, with his visitors.

Hugh You and I have already met, sir.

Lancey Yes.

Owen And Lieutenant Yolland – both Royal Engineers – my father.

Hugh You're very welcome, gentlemen.

Yolland How do you do.

Hugh *Gaudeo vos hic adesse.*

Owen And I'll make no other introductions except that these are some of the people of Baile Beag and – what? – well you're among the best people in Ireland now.

He pauses to allow Lancey to speak. Lancey does not.

Would you like to say a few words, Captain?

Hugh What about a drop, sir?

Lancey A what?

Hugh Perhaps a modest refreshment? A little sampling of our aqua vitae?

Lancey No, no.

Hugh Later perhaps when ...

Lancey I'll say what I have to say, if I may, and as briefly as possible. Do they speak *any* English, Roland?

Owen Don't worry. I'll translate.

Lancey I see. (*He clears his throat. He speaks as if he were addressing children – a shade too loudly and enunciating excessively.*) You may have seen me – seen me – working in this section – section? – working. We are here – here – in this place – you understand? – to make a map – a map – a map and –

Jimmy *Nonne Latine loquitur?*

Hugh holds up a restraining hand.

Hugh James.

Lancey (*to Jimmy*) I do not speak Gaelic, sir. (*He looks at Owen.*)

Owen Carry on.

Lancey A map is a representation on paper – a picture – you understand picture? – a paper picture – showing, representing this country – yes? – showing your country in miniature – a scaled drawing on paper of – of – of –

Suddenly Doalty sniggers. Then Bridget. Then Sarah. Owen leaps in quickly.

Owen It might be better if you *assume* they understand you –

Lancey Yes?

Owen And I'll translate as you go along.

Lancey I see. Yes. Very well. Perhaps you're right. Well. What we are doing is this.

He looks at Owen. Owen nods reassuringly.

His Majesty's government has ordered the first ever comprehensive survey of this entire country – a general triangulation which will embrace detailed hydrographic and topographic information and which will be executed to a scale of six inches to the English mile.

Hugh (*pouring a drink*) Excellent – excellent.

Lancey looks at Owen.

Owen A new map is being made of the whole country.

Lancey looks to Owen: Is that all? Owen smiles reassuringly and indicates to proceed.

Lancey This enormous task has been embarked on so that

the military authorities will be equipped with up-to-date and accurate information on every corner of this part of the Empire.

Owen The job is being done by soldiers because they are skilled in this work.

Lancey And also so that the entire basis of land valuation can be reassessed for purposes of more equitable taxation.

Owen This new map will take the place of the estate-agent's map so that from now on you will know exactly what is yours in law.

Lancey In conclusion I wish to quote two brief extracts from the white paper which is our governing charter: (*Reads.*) 'All former surveys of Ireland originated in forfeiture and violent transfer of property; the present survey has for its object the relief which can be afforded to the proprietors and occupiers of land from unequal taxation.'

Owen The captain hopes that the public will cooperate with the sappers and that the new map will mean that taxes are reduced.

Hugh A worthy enterprise – *opus honestum*! And Extract B?

Lancey 'Ireland is privileged. No such survey is being undertaken in England. So this survey cannot but be received as proof of the disposition of this government to advance the interests of Ireland.' My sentiments, too.

Owen This survey demonstrates the government's interest in Ireland and the captain thanks you for listening so attentively to him.

Hugh Our pleasure, Captain.

Lancey Lieutenant Yolland?

Yolland I – I – I've nothing to say – really –

Owen The captain is the man who actually makes the new map. George's task is to see that the place-names on this map are ... correct. (*to Yolland.*) Just a few words – they'd like to hear you. (*to class*) Don't you want to hear George, too?

Maire Has he anything to say?

Yolland (*to Maire*) Sorry – sorry?

Owen She says she's dying to hear you.

Yolland (*to Maire*) Very kind of you – thank you ... (*to class*) I can only say that I feel – I feel very foolish to – to – to be working here and not to speak your language. But I intend to rectify that – with Roland's help – indeed I do.

Owen He wants me to teach him Irish!

Hugh You are doubly welcome, sir.

Yolland I think your countryside is – is – is – is very beautiful. I've fallen in love with it already. I hope we're not too – too crude an intrusion on your lives. And I know that I'm going to be happy, very happy, here.

Owen He is already a committed Hibernophile –

Jimmy He loves –

Owen All right, Jimmy – we know – he loves Baile Beag; and he loves you all.

Hugh Please ... May I ...?

Hugh is now drunk. He holds on to the edge of the table.

Owen Go ahead, Father. (*hands up for quiet*) Please – please.

Hugh And we, gentlemen, we in turn are happy to offer you our friendship, our hospitality, and every assistance that you may require. Gentlemen – welcome!

A few desultory claps. The formalities are over. General conversation. The soldiers meet the locals.
Manus and Owen meet down stage.

Owen Lancey's a bloody ramrod but George's all right. How are you anyway?

Manus What sort of a translation was that, Owen?

Owen Did I make a mess of it?

Manus You weren't saying what Lancey was saying!

Owen 'Uncertainty in meaning is incipient poetry' – who said that?

Manus There was nothing uncertain about what Lancey said: it's a bloody military operation, Owen! And what's Yolland's function? What's 'incorrect' about the place-names we have here?

Owen Nothing at all. They're just going to be standardised.

Manus You mean changed into English?

Owen Where there's ambiguity, they'll be Anglicised.

Manus And they call you Roland! They both call you Roland!

Owen Shhhhh. Isn't it ridiculous? They seem to get it wrong from the very beginning – or else they can't pronounce Owen. I was afraid some of you bastards would laugh.

Manus Aren't you going to tell them?

Owen Yes – yes – soon – soon.

Manus But they ...

Owen Easy, man, easy. Owen – Roland – what the hell. It's only a name. It's the same me, isn't it? Well, isn't it?

Manus Indeed is it. It's the same Owen.

Owen And the same Manus. And in a way we complement each other. (*He punches Manus lightly, playfully, and turns to join the others. As he goes:*) All right – who has met whom? Isn't this a job for the go-between?

> *Manus watches Owen move confidently across the floor, taking Maire by the hand and introducing her to Yolland.*
> *Hugh is trying to negotiate the steps.*
> *Jimmy is lost in a text.*
> *Doalty and Bridget are reliving their giggling.*
> *Sarah is staring at Manus.*

Act Two

SCENE ONE

The sappers have already mapped most of the area. Yolland's official task, which Owen is now doing, is to take each of the Gaelic names – every hill, stream, rock, even every patch of ground which possessed its own distinctive Irish name – and Anglicise it, either by changing it into its approximate English sound or by translating it into English words. For example, a Gaelic name like Cnoc Ban could become Knockban or – directly translated – Fair Hill. These new standardised names were entered into the Name-Book, and when the new maps appeared they contained all these new Anglicised names. Owen's official function as translator is to pronounce each name in Irish and then provide the English translation.

The hot weather continues. It is late afternoon some days later.

Stage right: an improvised clothes-line strung between the shafts of the cart and a nail in the wall; on it are some shirts and socks.

A large map – one of the new blank maps – is spread out on the floor. Owen is on his hands and knees, consulting it. He is totally engrossed in his task which he pursues with great energy and efficiency.

Yolland's hesitancy has vanished – he is at home here now. He is sitting on the floor, his long legs stretched out before him, his back resting against a creel, his eyes closed. His mind is elsewhere. One of the reference books – a church registry – lies open on his lap.

Around them are various reference books, the Name-Book, a bottle of poteen, some cups etc.

Owen completes an entry in the Name-Book and returns to the map on the floor.

Owen Now. Where have we got to? Yes – the point where that stream enters the sea – that tiny little beach there. George!

Yolland Yes. I'm listening. What do you call it? Say the Irish name again?

Owen Bun na hAbhann.

Yolland Again.

Owen Bun na hAbhann.

Yolland Bun na hAbhann.

Owen That's terrible, George.

Yolland I know. I'm sorry. Say it again.

Owen Bun na hAbhann.

Yolland Bun na hAbhann.

Owen That's better. Bun is the Irish word for bottom. And Abha means river. So it's literally the mouth of the river.

Yolland Let's leave it alone. There's no English equivalent for a sound like that.

Owen What is it called in the church registry?

Only now does Yolland open his eyes.

Yolland Let's see ... Banowen.

Owen That's wrong. (*Consults text.*) The list of freeholders calls it Owenmore – that's completely wrong: Owenmore's the big river at the west end of the parish. (*another text*) And in the grand jury lists it's called – God! – Binhone! – wherever they got that. I suppose we could Anglicise it to Bunowen; but somehow that's neither fish nor flesh.

Yolland closes his eyes again.

Yolland I give up.

Owen (*at map*) Back to first principles. What are we trying to do?

Yolland Good question.

Owen We are trying to denominate and at the same time describe that tiny area of soggy, rocky, sandy ground where that little stream enters the sea, an area known locally as Bun na hAbhann ... Burnfoot! What about Burnfoot?

Yolland (*indifferently*) Good, Roland. Burnfoot's good.

Owen George, my name isn't ...

Yolland B-u-r-n-f-o-o-t?

Owen I suppose so. What do you think?

Yolland Yes.

Owen Are you happy with that?

Yolland Yes.

Owen Burnfoot it is then. (*He makes the entry into the Name-Book.*) Bun na hAbhann – B-u-r-n-

Yolland You're becoming very skilled at this.

Owen We're not moving fast enough.

Yolland (*opens eyes again*) Lancey lectured me again last night.

Owen When does he finish here?

Yolland The sappers are pulling out at the end of the week. The trouble is, the maps they've completed can't be printed without these names. So London screams at

Lancey and Lancey screams at me. But I wasn't intimidated.

Manus emerges from upstairs and descends.

'I'm sorry, sir,' I said, 'But certain tasks demand their own tempo. You cannot rename a whole country overnight.' Your Irish air has made me bold. (*to Manus*) Do you want us to leave?

Manus Time enough. Class won't begin for another half-hour.

Yolland Sorry – sorry?

Owen Can't you speak English?

Manus gathers the things off the clothes-line. Owen returns to the map.

We now come across that beach …

Yolland Tra – that's the Irish for beach. (*to Manus*) I'm picking up the odd word, Manus.

Manus So.

Owen … on past Burnfoot; and there's nothing around here that has any name that I know of until we come down here to the south end, just about here … and there should be a ridge of rocks there … Have the sappers marked it? They have. Look, George.

Yolland Where are we?

Owen There.

Yolland I'm lost.

Owen Here. And the name of that ridge is Druim Dubh. Put English on that, Lieutenant.

Yolland Say it again.

Owen Druim Dubh.

Yolland Dubh means black.

Owen Yes.

Yolland And Druim means ... what? a fort?

Owen We met it yesterday in Druim Luachra.

Yolland A ridge! The Black Ridge! (*to Manus*) You see, Manus?

Owen We'll have you fluent at the Irish before the summer's over.

Yolland Oh I wish I were. (*To Manus as he crosses to go back upstairs.*) We got a crate of oranges from Dublin today. I'll send some up to you.

Manus Thanks. (*to Owen*) Better hide that bottle. Father's just up and he'd be better without it.

Owen Can't you speak English before your man?

Manus Why?

Owen Out of courtesy.

Manus Doesn't he want to learn Irish? (*to Yolland*) Don't you want to learn Irish?

Yolland Sorry – sorry? I – I –

Manus I understand the Lanceys perfectly but people like you puzzle me.

Owen Manus, for God's sake!

Manus (*still to Yolland*) How's the work going?

Yolland The work? – the work? Oh, it's – it's staggering along – I think – (*to Owen*) – isn't it? But we'd be lost without Roland.

Manus (*leaving*) I'm sure. But there are always the Rolands, aren't there? (*He goes upstairs and exits.*)

Yolland What was that he said? – something about Lancey, was it?

Owen He said we should hide that bottle before Father gets his hands on it.

Yolland Ah.

Owen He's always trying to protect him.

Yolland Was he lame from birth?

Owen An accident when he was a baby: Father fell across his cradle. That's why Manus feels so responsible for him.

Yolland Why doesn't he marry?

Owen Can't afford to, I suppose.

Yolland Hasn't he a salary?

Owen What salary? All he gets is the odd shilling Father throws him – and that's seldom enough. I got out in time, didn't I?

Yolland is pouring a drink.

Easy with that stuff – it'll hit you suddenly.

Yolland I like it.

Owen Let's get back to the job. Druim Dubh – what's it called in the jury lists? (*Consults texts.*)

Yolland Some people here resent us.

Owen Dramduff – wrong as usual.

Yolland I was passing a little girl yesterday and she spat at me.

Owen And it's Drimdoo here. What's it called in the registry?

Yolland Do you know the Donnelly twins?

Owen Who?

Yolland The Donnelly twins.

Owen Yes. Best fishermen about here. What about them?

Yolland Lancey's looking for them.

Owen What for?

Yolland He wants them for questioning.

Owen Probably stolen somebody's nets. Dramduffy! Nobody ever called it Dramduffy. Take your pick of those three.

Yolland My head's addled. Let's take a rest. Do you want a drink?

Owen Thanks. Now, every Dubh we've come across we've changed to Duff. So if we're to be consistent, I suppose Druim Dubh has to become Dromduff.

Yolland is now looking out the window.

You can see the end of the ridge from where you're standing. But D-r-u-m or D-r-o-m? (*Name-Book*) Do you remember – which did we agree on for Druim Luachra?

Yolland That house immediately above where we're camped –

Owen Mm?

Yolland The house where Maire lives.

Owen Maire? Oh, Maire Chatach.

Yolland What does that mean?

Owen Curly-haired; the whole family are called the Catachs. What about it?

Yolland I hear music coming from that house almost every night.

Owen Why don't you drop in?

Yolland Could I?

Owen Why not? We used D-r-o-m then. So we've got to call it D-r-o-m-d-u-f-f – all right?

Yolland Go back up to where the new school is being built and just say the names again for me, would you?

Owen That's a good idea. Poolkerry, Bally Beg –

Yolland No, no; as they still are – in your own language.

Owen Poll na gCaorach,

Yolland repeats the names silently after him.

Baile Beag, Ceann Balor, Lis Maol, Machaire Buidhe, Baile na gCall, Carraig na Ri, Mullach Dearg –

Yolland Do you think I could live here?

Owen What are you talking about?

Yolland Settle down here – live here.

Owen Come on, George.

Yolland I mean it.

Owen Live on what? Potatoes? Buttermilk?

Yolland It's really heavenly.

Owen For God's sake! The first hot summer in fifty years and you think it's Eden. Don't be such a bloody romantic. You wouldn't survive a mild winter here.

Yolland Do you think not? Maybe you're right.

Doalty enters in a rush.

Doalty Hi, boys, is Manus about?

Owen He's upstairs. Give him a shout.

Doalty Manus!
The cattle's going mad in that heat – Cripes, running wild all over the place. (*to Yolland*) How are you doing, skipper?

Manus appears.

Yolland Thank you for – I – I'm very grateful to you for –

Doalty Wasting your time. I don't know a word you're saying. Hi, Manus, there's two bucks down the road there asking for you.

Manus (*descending*) Who are they?

Doalty Never clapped eyes on them. They want to talk to you.

Manus What about?

Doalty They wouldn't say. Come on. The bloody beasts'll end up in Loch an Iubhair if they're not capped. Good luck, boys!

Doalty rushes off. Manus follows him.

Owen Good luck! What were you thanking Doalty for?

Yolland I was washing outside my tent this morning and he was passing with a scythe across his shoulder and he came up to me and pointed to the long grass and then cut a pathway round my tent and from the tent down to the road – so that my feet won't get wet with the dew. Wasn't that kind of him? And I have no words to thank him ... I suppose you're right: I suppose I couldn't live here ... Just before Doalty came up to me this morning, I was thinking that at that moment I might have been in Bombay instead of Ballybeg. You see, my father was at his wits' end with me and finally he got me a job with the East India Company – some kind of clerkship. This was ten, eleven months ago. So I set off for London. Unfortunately I – I – I missed the boat. Literally. And since I couldn't face Father and hadn't enough money to hang about until the next sailing, I joined the Army. And they stuck me into the Engineers and posted me to Dublin. And Dublin sent me here. And while I was washing this morning and looking across the Tra Bhan, I was thinking how very, very lucky I am to be here and not in Bombay.

Owen Do you believe in fate?

Yolland Lancey's so like my father. I was watching him last night. He met every group of sappers as they reported in. He checked the field kitchens. He examined the horses. He inspected every single report – even examining the texture of the paper and commenting on the neatness of the handwriting. The perfect colonial servant: not only must the job be done – it must be done with excellence. Father has that drive, too; that dedication; that indefatigable energy. He builds roads – hopping from one end of the Empire to the other. Can't sit still for five minutes. He says himself the longest time he ever sat still was the night before Waterloo when they were waiting for Wellington to make up his mind to attack.

Owen What age is he?

Yolland Born in 1789 – the very day the Bastille fell. I've often thought maybe that gave his whole life its character. Do you think it could? He inherited a new world the day he was born – the Year One. Ancient time was at an end. The world had cast off its old skin. There were no longer any frontiers to man's potential. Possibilities were endless and exciting. He still believes that. The Apocalypse is just about to happen ... I'm afraid I'm a great disappointment to him. I've neither his energy, nor his coherence, nor his belief. Do I believe in fate? The day I arrived in Ballybeg –

no, Baile Beag – the moment you brought me in here, I had a curious sensation. It's difficult to describe. It was a momentary sense of discovery; no – not quite a sense of discovery – a sense of recognition, of confirmation of something I half knew instinctively; as if I had stepped ...

Owen Back into ancient time?

Yolland No, no. It wasn't an awareness of *direction* being changed but of experience being of a totally different order. I had moved into a consciousness that wasn't striving nor agitated, but at its ease and with its own conviction and assurance. And when I heard Jimmy Jack and your father swapping stories about Apollo and Cuchulainn and Paris and Ferdia – as if they lived down the road – it was then that I thought – I knew – perhaps I could live here ... (*now embarrassed*) Where's the pot-een?

Owen Poteen?

Yolland Poteen – poteen – poteen. Even if I did speak Irish I'd always be an outsider here, wouldn't I? I may learn the password but the language of the tribe will always elude me, won't it? The private core will always be ... hermetic, won't it?

Owen You can learn to decode us.

Hugh emerges from upstairs and descends. He is dressed for the road. Today he is physically and mentally jaunty and alert – almost self-consciously jaunty and alert. Indeed, as the scene progresses, one has the sense that he is deliberately parodying himself.

The moment Hugh gets to the bottom of the steps Yolland leaps respectfully to his feet.

Hugh (*as he descends*)
Quantumvis cursum longum fessumque moratur
Sol, sacro tandem carmine vesper adest.

I dabble in verse, Lieutenant, after the style of Ovid. (*to Owen*) A drop of that to fortify me.

Yolland You'll have to translate it for me.

Hugh Let's see –
No matter how long the sun may linger on his long and weary journey
At length evening comes with its sacred song.

Yolland Very nice, sir.

Hugh English succeeds in making it sound ... plebeian.

Owen Where are you off to, Father?

Hugh An *expeditio* with three purposes. Purpose A: to acquire a testimonial from our parish priest – (*to Yolland*) a worthy man but barely literate; and since he'll ask me to write it myself, how in all modesty can I do myself justice? (*to Owen*) Where did this (*drink*) come from?

Owen Anna na mBreag's.

Hugh (*to Yolland*) In that case address yourself to it with circumspection. (*And he instantly tosses the drink back in one gulp and grimaces. (Aaaaaaagh!) Holds out his glass for a refill.*) Anna na mBreag means Anna of the Lies. And Purpose B: to talk to the builders of the new school about the kind of living accommodation I will require there. I have lived too long like a journeyman tailor.

Yolland Some years ago we lived fairly close to a poet – well, about three miles away.

Hugh His name?

Yolland Wordsworth – William Wordsworth.

Hugh Did he speak of me to you?

Yolland Actually I never talked to him. I just saw him out walking – in the distance.

Hugh Wordsworth? ... no. I'm afraid we're not familiar with your literature, Lieutenant. We feel closer to the warm Mediterranean. We tend to overlook your island.

Yolland I'm learning to speak Irish, sir.

Hugh Good.

Yolland Roland's teaching me.

Hugh Splendid.

Yolland I mean – I feel so cut off from the people here. And I was trying to explain a few minutes ago how remarkable a community this is. To meet people like yourself and Jimmy Jack who actually converse in Greek and Latin. And your place names – what was the one we came across this morning? – Termon, from Terminus, the god of boundaries. It – it – it's really astonishing.

Hugh We like to think we endure around truths immemorially posited.

Yolland And your Gaelic literature – you're a poet yourself –

Hugh Only in Latin, I'm afraid.

Yolland I understand it's enormously rich and ornate.

Hugh Indeed, Lieutenant. A rich language. A rich literature. You'll find, sir, that certain cultures expend on their vocabularies and syntax acquisitive energies and ostentations entirely lacking in their material lives. I suppose you could call us a spiritual people.

Owen (*not unkindly; more out of embarrassment before Yolland*) Will you stop that nonsense, Father.

Hugh Nonsense? What nonsense?

Owen Do you know where the priest lives?

Hugh At Lis na Muc, over near...

Owen No, he doesn't. Lis na Muc, the Fort of the Pigs, has become Swinefort. (*Now turning the pages of the Name-Book – a page per name.*) And to get to Swinefort you pass through Greencastle and Fair Head and Strandhill and Gort and Whiteplains. And the new school isn't at Poll na gCaorach – it's at Sheepsrock. Will you be able to find your way?

Hugh pours himself another drink. Then:

Hugh Yes, it is a rich language, Lieutenant, full of the mythologies of fantasy and hope and self-deception – a syntax opulent with tomorrows. It is our response to mud cabins and a diet of potatoes; our only method of replying to ... inevitabilities. (*to Owen*) Can you give me the loan of half-a-crown? I'll repay you out of the subscriptions I'm collecting for the publication of my new book. (*to Yolland*) It is entitled: 'The Pentaglot Preceptor or Elementary Institute of the English, Greek, Hebrew, Latin and Irish Languages; Particularly Calculated for the Instruction of Such Ladies and Gentlemen as may Wish to Learn without the Help of a Master'.

Yolland (*laughs*) That's a wonderful title!

Hugh Between ourselves – the best part of the enterprise. Nor do I, in fact, speak Hebrew. And that last phrase – 'without the Help of a Master' – that was written before the new national school was thrust upon me – do you think I ought to drop it now? After all you don't dispose of the cow just because it has produced a magnificent calf, do you?

Yolland You certainly do not.

Hugh The phrase goes. And I'm interrupting work of moment. (*He goes to the door and stops there.*) To return

briefly to that other matter, Lieutenant. I understand your sense of exclusion, of being cut off from a life here; and I trust you will find access to us with my son's help. But remember that words are signals, counters. They are not immortal. And it can happen – to use an image you'll understand – it can happen that a civilisation can be imprisoned in a linguistic contour which no longer matches the landscape of ... fact.
Gentlemen. (*He leaves.*)

Owen 'An *expeditio* with three purposes': the children laugh at him: he always promises three points and he never gets beyond A and B.

Yolland He's an astute man.

Owen He's bloody pompous.

Yolland But so astute.

Owen And he drinks too much. Is it astute not to be able to adjust for survival? Enduring around truths immemorially posited – hah!

Yolland He knows what's happening.

Owen What is happening?

Yolland I'm not sure. But I'm concerned about my part in it. It's an eviction of sorts.

Owen We're making a six-inch map of the country. Is there something sinister in that?

Yolland Not in ...

Owen And we're taking place-names that are riddled with confusion and ...

Yolland Who's confused? Are the people confused?

Owen ... and we're standardising those names as accurately and as sensitively as we can.

Yolland Something is being eroded.

Owen Back to the romance again. All right! Fine! Fine! Look where we've got to. (*He drops on his hands and knees and stabs a finger at the map.*) We've come to this crossroads. Come here and look at it, man! Look at it! And we call that crossroads Tobair Vree. And why do we call it Tobair Vree? I'll tell you why. Tobair means a well. But what does Vree mean? It's a corruption of Brian – (*Gaelic pronunciation*) Brian – an erosion of Tobair Bhriain. Because a hundred-and-fifty years ago there used to be a well there, not at the crossroads, mind you – that would be too simple – but in a field close to the crossroads. And an old man called Brian, whose face was disfigured by an enormous growth, got it into his head that the water in that well was blessed; and every day for seven months he went there and bathed his face in it. But the growth didn't go away; and one morning Brian was found drowned in that well. And ever since that crossroads is known as Tobair Vree – even though that well has long since dried up. I know the story because my grandfather told it to me. But ask Doalty – or Maire – or Bridget – even my father – even Manus – why it's called Tobair Vree; and do you think they'll know? I know they don't know. So the question I put to you, Lieutenant, is this: what do we do with a name like that? Do we scrap Tobair Vree altogether and call it – what? – The Cross? Crossroads? Or do we keep piety with a man long dead, long forgotten, his name 'eroded' beyond recognition, whose trivial little story nobody in the parish remembers?

Yolland Except you.

Owen I've left here.

Yolland You remember it.

Owen I'm asking you: what do we write in the Name-Book?

Yolland Tobair Vree.

Owen Even though the well is a hundred yards from the actual crossroads – and there's no well anyway – and what the hell does Vree mean?

Yolland Tobair Vree.

Owen That's what you want?

Yolland Yes.

Owen You're certain?

Yolland Yes.

Owen Fine. Fine. That's what you'll get.

Yolland That's what you want, too, Roland.

Pause.

Owen (*explodes*) George! For God's sake! *My name is not Roland!*

Yolland What?

Owen (*softly*) My name is Owen.

Pause.

Yolland Not Roland?

Owen Owen.

Yolland You mean to say – ?

Owen Owen.

Yolland But I've been –

Owen O-w-e-n.

Yolland Where did Roland come from?

Owen I don't know.

Yolland It was never Roland?

Owen Never.

Yolland O my God!

Pause. They stare at one another. Then the absurdity of the situation strikes them suddenly. They explode with laughter. Owen pours drinks. As they roll about their lines overlap.

Yolland Why didn't you tell me?

Owen Do I look like a Roland?

Yolland Spell Owen again.

Owen I was getting fond of Roland.

Yolland O my God!

Owen O-w-e-n.

Yolland What'll we write –

Owen – in the Name-Book?

Yolland R-o-w-e-n!

Owen Or what about Ol-

Yolland Ol- what?

Owen Oland!

And again they explode.
Manus enters. He is very elated.

Manus What's the celebration?

Owen A christening!

Yolland A baptism!

Owen A hundred christenings!

Yolland A thousand baptisms! Welcome to Eden!

Owen Eden's right! We name a thing and – bang! it leaps into existence!

Yolland Each name a perfect equation with its roots.

Owen A perfect congruence with its reality. (*to Manus*) Take a drink.

Yolland Poteen – beautiful.

Owen Lying Anna's poteen.

Yolland Anna na mBreag's poteen.

Owen Excellent, George.

Yolland I'll decode you yet.

Owen (*offers drink*) Manus?

Manus Not if that's what it does to you.

Owen You're right. Steady – steady – sober up – sober up.

Yolland Sober as a judge, Owen.

Manus moves beside Owen.

Manus I've got good news! Where's Father?

Owen He's gone out. What's the good news?

Manus I've been offered a job.

Owen Where? (*now aware of Yolland*) Come on, man – speak in English.

Manus For the benefit of the colonist?

Owen He's a decent man.

Manus Aren't they all at some level?

Owen Please.

Manus shrugs.

He's been offered a job.

Yolland Where?

Owen Well – tell us!

Manus I've just had a meeting with two men from Inis Meadhon. They want me to go there and start a hedge-school. They're giving me a free house, free turf, and free milk; a rood of standing corn; twelve drills of potatoes; and – (*He stops.*)

Owen And what?

Manus A salary of £42 a year!

Owen Manus, that's wonderful!

Manus You're talking to a man of substance.

Owen I'm delighted.

Yolland Where's Inis Meadhon?

Owen An island south of here. And they came looking for you?

Manus Well, I mean to say ...

Owen punches Manus.

Owen Aaaaagh! This calls for a real celebration.

Yolland Congratulations.

Manus Thank you.

Owen Where are you, Anna?

Yolland When do you start?

Manus Next Monday.

Owen We'll stay with you when we're there. (*to Yolland*) How long will it be before we reach Inis Meadhon?

Yolland How far south is it?

Manus About fifty miles.

Yolland Could we make it by December?

Owen We'll have Christmas together. (*Sings.*) 'Christmas Day on Inis Meadhon ...'

Yolland (*toast*) I hope you're very content there, Manus.

Manus Thank you.

Yolland holds out his hand. Manus takes it. They shake warmly.

Owen (*toast*) Manus.

Manus (*toast*) To Inis Meadhon. (*He drinks quickly and turns to leave.*)

Owen Hold on – hold on – refills coming up.

Manus I've got to go.

Owen Come on, man; this is an occasion. Where are you rushing to?

Manus I've got to tell Maire.

Maire enters with her can of milk.

Maire You've got to tell Maire what?

Owen He's got a job!

Maire Manus?

Owen He's been invited to start a hedge-school in Inis Meadhon.

Maire Where?

Manus Inis Meadhon – the island! They're giving me £42 a year and ...

Owen A house, fuel, milk, potatoes, corn, pupils, what-not!

Manus I start on Monday.

Owen You'll take a drink. Isn't it great?

Manus I want to talk to you for...

Maire There's your milk. I need the can back.

Manus takes the can and runs up the steps.

Manus (*as he goes*) How will you like living on an island?

Owen You know George, don't you?

Maire We wave to each other across the fields.

Yolland Sorry-sorry?

Owen She says you wave to each other across the fields.

Yolland Yes, we do; oh yes, indeed we do.

Maire What's he saying?

Owen He says you wave to each other across the fields.

Maire That's right. So we do.

Yolland What's she saying?

Owen Nothing – nothing — nothing. (*to Maire*) What's the news?

Maire moves away, touching the text books with her toe.

Maire Not a thing. You're busy, the two of you.

Owen We think we are.

Maire I hear the Fiddler O'Shea's about. There's some talk of a dance tomorrow night.

Owen Where will it be?

Maire Maybe over the road. Maybe at Tobair Vree.

Yolland Tobair Vree!

Maire Yes.

Yolland Tobair Vree! Tobair Vree!

Maire Does he know what I'm saying?

Owen Not a word.

Maire Tell him then.

Owen Tell him what?

Maire About the dance.

Owen Maire says there may be a dance tomorrow night.

Yolland (*to Owen*) Yes? May I come?
(*to Maire*) Would anybody object if I came?

Maire (*to Owen*) What's he saying?

Owen (*to Yolland*) Who would object?

Maire (*to Owen*) Did you tell him?

Yolland (*to Maire*) Sorry-sorry?

Owen (*to Maire*) He says may he come?

Maire (*to Yolland*) That's up to you.

Yolland (*to Owen*) What does she say?

Owen (*to Yolland*) She says –

Yolland (*to Maire*) What-what?

Maire (*to Owen*) Well?

Yolland (*to Owen*) Sorry-sorry?

Owen (*to Yolland*) Will you go?

Yolland (*to Maire*) Yes, yes, if I may.

Maire (*to Owen*) What does he say?

Yolland (*to Owen*) What is she saying?

Owen O for God's sake! (*To Manus who is descending with the empty can.*) You take on this job, Manus.

Manus I'll walk you up to the house. Is your mother at home? I want to talk to her.

Maire What's the rush? (*to Owen*) Didn't you offer me a drink?

Owen Will you risk Anna na mBreag?

Maire Why not.

Yolland is suddenly intoxicated. He leaps up on a stool, raises his glass and shouts.

Yolland Anna na mBreag! Baile Beag! Inis Meadhon! Bombay! Tobair Vree! Eden! And poteen – correct, Owen?

Owen Perfect.

Yolland And bloody marvellous stuff it is, too. I love it! Bloody, bloody, bloody marvellous!

Simultaneously with his final 'bloody marvellous' bring up very loud the introductory music of the reel. Then immediately go to black. Retain the music throughout the very brief interval.

SCENE TWO

The following night.
This scene may be played in the schoolroom, but it would be preferable to lose – by lighting – as much of the

schoolroom as possible, and to play the scene down front in a vaguely 'outside' area.

The music rises to a crescendo. Then in the distance we hear Maire and Yolland approach – laughing and running. They run on, hand-in-hand. They have just left the dance.

Fade the music to distant background. Then after a time it is lost and replaced by guitar music.

Maire and Yolland are now down front, still holding hands and excited by their sudden and impetuous escape from the dance.

Maire O my God, that leap across the ditch nearly killed me.

Yolland I could scarcely keep up with you.

Maire Wait till I get my breath back.

Yolland We must have looked as if we were being chased.

They now realise they are alone and holding hands – the beginnings of embarrassment. The hands disengage. They begin to drift apart. Pause.

Maire Manus'll wonder where I've got to.

Yolland I wonder did anyone notice us leave.

Pause. Slightly further apart.

Maire The grass must be wet. My feet are soaking.

Yolland Your feet must be wet. The grass is soaking.

Another pause. Another few paces apart. They are now a long distance from one another.

(*Indicating himself.*) George.

Maire nods: Yes – yes. Then:

Maire Lieutenant George.

Yolland Don't call me that. I never think of myself as Lieutenant.

Maire What-what?

Yolland Sorry-sorry? (*He points to himself again.*) George.

Maire nods: Yes-yes. Then points to herself.

Maire Maire.

Yolland Yes, I know you're Maire. Of course I know you're Maire. I mean I've been watching you night and day for the past ...

Maire (*eagerly*) What-what?

Yolland (*points*) Maire. (*Points.*) George. (*Points both.*) Maire and George.

Maire nods: Yes-yes-yes.

I – I – I –

Maire Say anything at all. I love the sound of your speech.

Yolland (*eagerly*) Sorry-sorry?

In acute frustration he looks around, hoping for some inspiration that will provide him with communicative means. Now he has a thought: he tries raising his voice and articulating in a staccato style and with equal and absurd emphasis on each word.

Every-morning-I-see-you-feeding-brown-hens-and-giving-meal-to-black-calf – (*the futility of it*) – O my God.

Maire smiles. She moves towards him. She will try to communicate in Latin.

Maire *Tu es centurio in – in – in exercitu Britannico –*

Yolland Yes-yes? Go on – go on – say anything at all – I love the sound of your speech.

Maire – *et es in castris quae – quae – quae sunt in agro –* (*the futility of it*) – O my God.

> *Yolland smiles. He moves towards her. Now for her English words.*

George – water.

Yolland 'Water'? Water! Oh yes – water – water – very good – water – good – good.

Maire Fire.

Yolland Fire – indeed – wonderful – fire, fire, fire – splendid – splendid!

Maire Ah ... ah ...

Yolland Yes? Go on.

Maire Earth.

Yolland 'Earth'?

Maire Earth. Earth.

> *Yolland still does not understand.*
> *Maire stoops down and picks up a handful of clay. Holding it out*

Earth.

Yolland Earth! Of course – earth! Earth. Earth. Good Lord, Maire, your English is perfect!

Maire (*eagerly*) What-what?

Yolland Perfect English. English perfect.

Maire George –

Yolland That's beautiful – oh that's really beautiful.

Maire George –

Yolland Say it again – say it again –

Maire Shhh. (*She holds her hand up for silence – she is trying to remember her one line of English. Now she remembers it and she delivers the line as if English were her language – easily, fluidly, conversationally.* George, in Norfolk we besport ourselves around the maypoll.

Yolland Good God, do you? That's where my mother comes from – Norfolk. Norwich actually. Not exactly Norwich town but a small village called Little Walsingham close beside it. But in our own village of Winfarthing we have a maypole too and every year on the first of May –

He stops abruptly, only now realising. He stares at her. She in turn misunderstands his excitement.

Maire (*to herself*) Mother of God, my Aunt Mary wouldn't have taught me something dirty, would she?

Pause.
  Yolland extends his hand to Maire. She turns away from him and moves slowly across the stage.

Yolland Maire.

She still moves away.

Maire Chatach.

She still moves away.

Bun na hAbhann? (*He says the name softly, almost privately, very tentatively, as if he were searching for a sound she might respond to. He tries again.*) Druim Dubh?

Maire stops. She is listening. Yolland is encouraged.

Poll na gCaorach. Lis Maol.

Maire turns towards him.

Lis na nGall.

Maire Lis na nGradh.

They are now facing each other and begin moving – almost imperceptibly – towards one another.

Carraig an Phoill.

Yolland Carraig na Ri. Loch na nEan.

Maire Loch an Iubhair. Machaire Buidhe.

Yolland Machaire Mor. Cnoc na Mona.

Maire Cnoc na nGabhar.

Yolland Mullach.

Maire Port.

Yolland Tor.

Maire Lag.

She holds out her hands to Yolland. He takes them. Each now speaks almost to himself/herself.

Yolland I wish to God you could understand me.

Maire Soft hands; a gentleman's hands.

Yolland Because if you could understand me I could tell you how I spend my days either thinking of you or gazing up at your house in the hope that you'll appear even for a second.

Maire Every evening you walk by yourself along the Tra Bhan and every morning you wash yourself in front of your tent.

Yolland I would tell you how beautiful you are, curly-headed Maire. I would so like to tell you how beautiful you are.

Maire Your arms are long and thin and the skin on your shoulders is very white.

Yolland I would tell you ...

Maire Don't stop – I know what you're saying.

Yolland I would tell you how I want to be here – to live here – always – with you – always, always.

Maire 'Always'? What is that word – 'always'?

Yolland Yes-yes; always.

Maire You're trembling.

Yolland Yes, I'm trembling because of you.

Maire I'm trembling, too. (*She holds his face in her hand.*)

Yolland I've made up my mind ...

Maire Shhhh.

Yolland I'm not going to leave here ...

Maire Shhh – listen to me. I want you, too, soldier.

Yolland Don't stop – I know what you're saying.

Maire I want to live with you – anywhere – anywhere at all – always – always.

Yolland 'Always'? What is that word – 'always'?

Maire Take me away with you, George.

> *Pause.*
> *Suddenly they kiss.*
> *Sarah enters. She sees them. She stands shocked, staring at them. Her mouth works. Then almost to herself.*

Sarah Manus ... Manus!

> *Sarah runs off.*
> *Music to crescendo.*

Act Three

The following evening. It is raining.

Sarah and Owen alone in the schoolroom. Sarah, more waiflike than ever, is sitting very still on a stool, an open book across her knee. She is pretending to read but her eyes keep going up to the room upstairs. Owen is working on the floor as before, surrounded by his reference books, map, Name-Book etc. But he has neither concentration nor interest; and like Sarah he glances up at the upstairs room.

After a few seconds Manus emerges and descends, carrying a large paper bag which already contains his clothes. His movements are determined and urgent. He moves around the classroom, picking up books, examining each title carefully, and choosing about six of them which he puts into his bag. As he selects these books:

Owen You know that old limekiln beyond Con Connie Tim's pub, the place we call The Murren? – do you know why it's called The Murren?

Manus does not answer.

I've only just discovered: it's a corruption of Saint Muranus. It seems Saint Muranus had a monastery somewhere about there at the beginning of the seventh century. And over the years the name became shortened to the Murren. Very unattractive name, isn't it? I think we should go back to the original – Saint Muranus. What do you think? The original's Saint Muranus. Don't you think we should go back to that?

No response. Owen begins writing the name into the

Name-Book. Manus is now rooting about among the forgotten implements for a piece of rope. He finds a piece. He begins to tie the mouth of the flimsy, overloaded bag – and it bursts, the contents spilling out on the floor.

Manus Bloody, bloody, bloody hell!

His voice breaks in exasperation: he is about to cry. Owen leaps to his feet.

Owen Hold on. I've a bag upstairs.

He runs upstairs. Sarah waits until Owen is off. Then.

Sarah Manus ... Manus, I ...

Manus hears Sarah but makes no acknowledgement. He gathers up his belongings.
Owen reappears with the bag he had on his arrival.

Owen Take this one – I'm finished with it anyway. And it's supposed to keep out the rain.

Manus transfers his few belongings. Owen drifts back to his task. The packing is now complete.

Manus You'll be here for a while? For a week or two anyhow?

Owen Yes.

Manus You're not leaving with the army?

Owen I haven't made up my mind. Why?

Manus Those Inis Meadhon men will be back to see why I haven't turned up. Tell them – tell them I'll write to them as soon as I can. Tell them I still want the job but that it might be three or four months before I'm free to go.

Owen You're being damned stupid, Manus.

Manus Will you do that for me?

Owen Clear out now and Lancey'll think you're involved somehow.

Manus Will you do that for me?

Owen Wait a couple of days even. You know George – he's a bloody romantic – maybe he's gone out to one of the islands and he'll suddenly reappear tomorrow morning. Or maybe the search party'll find him this evening lying drunk somewhere in the sandhills. You've seen him drinking that poteen – doesn't know how to handle it. Had he drink on him last night at the dance?

Manus I had a stone in my hand when I went out looking for him – I was going to fell him. The lame scholar turned violent.

Owen Did anybody see you?

Manus (*again close to tears*) But when I saw him standing there at the side of the road – smiling – and her face buried in his shoulder – I couldn't even go close to them. I just shouted something stupid – something like, 'You're a bastard, Yolland.' If I'd even said it in English ... 'cos he kept saying 'Sorry-sorry?' The wrong gesture in the wrong language.

Owen And you didn't see him again?

Manus 'Sorry?'

Owen Before you leave tell Lancey that – just to clear yourself.

Manus What have I to say to Lancey? You'll give that message to the islandmen?

Owen I'm warning you: run away now and you're bound to be ...

Manus (*to Sarah*) Will you give that message to the Inis Meadhon men?

Sarah I will.

Manus picks up an old sack and throws it across his shoulders.

Owen Have you any idea where you're going?

Manus Mayo, maybe. I remember Mother saying she had cousins somewhere away out in the Erris Peninsula. (*He picks up his bag.*) Tell father I took only the Virgil and the Caesar and the Aeschylus because they're mine anyway – I bought them with the money I got for that pet lamb I reared – do you remember that pet lamb? And tell him that Nora Dan never returned the dictionary and that she still owes him two-and-six for last quarter's reading – he always forgets those things.

Owen Yes.

Manus And his good shirt's ironed and hanging up in the press and his clean socks are in the butter-box under the bed.

Owen All right.

Manus And tell him I'll write.

Owen If Maire asks where you've gone ...?

Manus He'll need only half the amount of milk now, won't he? Even less than half – he usually takes his tea black. (*Pause.*) And when he comes in at night – you'll hear him; he makes a lot of noise – I usually come down and give him a hand up. Those stairs are dangerous without a banister. Maybe before you leave you'd get Big Ned Frank to put up some sort of a handrail. (*Pause.*) And if you can bake, he's very fond of soda bread.

Owen I can give you money. I'm wealthy. Do you know what they pay me? Two shillings a day for this – this – this –

Manus rejects the offer by holding out his hand.

Goodbye, Manus.

Manus and Owen shake hands.
Then Manus picks up his bag briskly and goes towards the door. He stops a few paces beyond Sarah, turns, comes back to her. He addresses her as he did in Act One but now without warmth or concern for her.

Manus What is your name? (*Pause.*) Come on. What is your name?

Sarah My name is Sarah.

Manus Just Sarah? Sarah what? (*Pause.*) Well?

Sarah Sarah Johnny Sally.

Manus And where do you live? Come on.

Sarah I live in Bun na hAbhann. (*She is now crying quietly.*)

Manus Very good, Sarah Johnny Sally. There's nothing to stop you now – nothing in the wide world. (*Pause. He looks down at her.*) It's all right – it's all right – you did no harm – you did no harm at all. (*He stoops over her and kisses the top of her head – as if in absolution. Then briskly to the door and off.*)

Owen Good luck, Manus!

Sarah (*quietly*) I'm sorry ... I'm sorry ... I'm so sorry, Manus ...

Owen tries to work but cannot concentrate. He begins folding up the map. As he does:

Owen Is there class this evening?

Sarah nods: yes.

I suppose Father knows. Where is he anyhow?

Sarah points.

Where?

Sarah mimes rocking a baby.

I don't understand – where?

Sarah repeats the mime and wipes away tears. Owen is still puzzled.

It doesn't matter. He'll probably turn up.

Bridget and Doalty enter, sacks over their heads against the rain. They are self-consciously noisier, more ebullient, more garrulous than ever – brimming over with excitement and gossip and brio.

Doalty You're missing the crack, boys! Cripes, you're missing the crack! Fifty more soldiers arrived an hour ago!

Bridget And they're spread out in a big line from Sean Neal's over to Lag and they're moving straight across the fields towards Cnoc na nGabhar!

Doalty Prodding every inch of the ground in front of them with their bayonets and scattering animals and hens in all directions!

Bridget And tumbling everything before them – fences, ditches, haystacks, turf-stacks!

Doalty They came to Barney Petey's field of corn – straight through it be God as if it was heather!

Bridget Not a blade of it left standing!

Doalty And Barney Petey just out of his bed and running

after them in his drawers: 'You hoors you! Get out of my corn, you hoors you!'

Bridget First time he ever ran in his life.

Doalty Too lazy, the wee get, to cut it when the weather was good.

Sarah begins putting out the seats.

Bridget Tell them about Big Hughie.

Doalty Cripes, if you'd seen your aul fella, Owen.

Bridget They were all inside in Anna na mBreag's pub – all the crowd from the wake –

Doalty And they hear the commotion and they all come out to the street –

Bridget Your father in front; the Infant Prodigy footless behind him!

Doalty And your aul fella, he sees the army stretched across the countryside –

Bridget O my God!

Doalty And Cripes he starts roaring at them!

Bridget 'Visigoths! Huns! Vandals!'

Doalty *'Ignari! Stulti! Rustici!'*

Bridget And wee Jimmy Jack jumping up and down and shouting, 'Thermopylae! Thermopylae!'

Doalty You never saw crack like it in your life, boys. Come away on out with me, Sarah, and you'll see it all.

Bridget Big Hughie's fit to take no class. Is Manus about?

Owen Manus is gone.

Bridget Gone where?

Owen He's left – gone away.

Doalty Where to?

Owen He doesn't know. Mayo, maybe.

Doalty What's on in Mayo?

Owen (*to Bridget*) Did you see George and Maire Chatach leave the dance last night?

Bridget We did. Didn't we, Doalty?

Owen Did you see Manus following them out?

Bridget I didn't see him going out but I saw him coming in by himself later.

Owen Did George and Maire come back to the dance?

Bridget No.

Owen Did you see them again?

Bridget He left her home. We passed them going up the back road – didn't we, Doalty?

Owen And Manus stayed till the end of the dance?

Doalty We know nothing. What are you asking us for?

Owen Because Lancey'll question me when he hears Manus's gone. (*back to Bridget*) That's the way George went home? By the back road? That's where you saw him?

Bridget Leave me alone, Owen. I know nothing about Yolland. If you want to know about Yolland, ask the Donnelly twins.

Silence. Doalty moves over to the window.

(*to Sarah*) He's a powerful fiddler, O'Shea, isn't he? He told our Seamus he'll come back for a night at Hallowe'en.

Owen goes to Doalty who looks resolutely out the window.

Owen What's this about the Donnellys? (*Pause.*) Were they about last night?

Doalty Didn't see them if they were. (*Begins whistling through his teeth.*)

Owen George is a friend of mine.

Doalty So.

Owen I want to know what's happened to him.

Doalty Couldn't tell you.

Owen What have the Donnelly twins to do with it? (*Pause.*) Doalty!

Doalty I know nothing, Owen – nothing at all – I swear to God. All I know is this: on my way to the dance I saw their boat beached at Port. It wasn't there on my way home, after I left Bridget. And that's all I know. As God's my judge. The half-dozen times I met him I didn't know a word he said to me; but he seemed a right enough sort ... (*with sudden excessive interest in the scene outside*) Cripes, they're crawling all over the place! Cripes, there's millions of them! Cripes, they're levelling the whole land!

Owen moves away.
  Maire enters. She is bareheaded and wet from the rain; her hair in disarray. She attempts to appear normal but she is in acute distress, on the verge of being distraught. She is carrying the milk-can.

Maire Honest to God, I must be going off my head. I'm half-way here and I think to myself, 'Isn't this can very light?' and I look into it and isn't it empty.

Owen It doesn't matter.

Maire How will you manage for tonight?

Owen We have enough.

Maire Are you sure?

Owen Plenty, thanks.

Maire It'll take me no time at all to go back up for some.

Owen Honestly, Maire.

Maire Sure it's better you have it than that black calf that's ... that ... (*She looks around.*) Have you heard anything?

Owen Nothing.

Maire What does Lancey say?

Owen I haven't seen him since this morning.

Maire What does he *think*?

Owen We really didn't talk. He was here for only a few seconds.

Maire He left me home, Owen. And the last thing he said to me – he tried to speak in Irish – he said, 'I'll see you yesterday' – he meant to say 'I'll see you tomorrow.' And I laughed that much he pretended to get cross and he said 'Maypoll! Maypoll!' because I said that word wrong. And off he went, laughing – laughing, Owen! Do you think he's all right? What do *you* think?

Owen I'm sure he'll turn up, Maire.

Maire He comes from a tiny wee place called Winfarthing. (*She suddenly drops on her hands and knees on the floor – where Owen had his map a few minutes ago – and with her finger traces out an outline map.*) Come here till you see. Look. There's Winfarthing. And there's two other wee villages right beside it; one of them's called

Barton Bendish – it's there; and the other's called
Saxingham Nethergate – it's about there. And there's Little
Walsingham – that's his mother's townland. Aren't they
odd names? Sure they make no sense to me at all. And
Winfarthing's near a big town called Norwich. And
Norwich is in a county called Norfolk. And Norfolk is in
the east of England. He drew a map for me on the wet
strand and wrote the names on it. I have it all in my head
now: Winfarthing – Barton Bendish – Saxingham
Nethergate – Little Walsingham – Norwich – Norfolk.
Strange sounds, aren't they? But nice sounds; like Jimmy
Jack reciting his Homer. (*She gets to her feet and looks
around; she is almost serene now.*) (*To Sarah*) You were
looking lovely last night, Sarah. Is that the dress you got
from Boston? Green suits you.
(*to Owen*) Something very bad's happened to him, Owen.
I know. He wouldn't go away without telling me. Where is
he, Owen? You're his friend – where is he? (*Again she
looks around the room; then sits on a stool.*) I didn't get a
chance to do my geography last night. The master'll be
angry with me. (*She rises again.*) I think I'll go home now.
The wee ones have to be washed and put to bed and that
black calf has to be fed ... My hands are that rough;
they're still blistered from the hay. I'm ashamed of them. I
hope to God there's no hay to be saved in Brooklyn. (*She
stops at the door.*) Did you hear? Nellie Ruadh's baby died
in the middle of the night. I must go up to the wake. It
didn't last long, did it?

Maire leaves. Silence. Then:

Owen I don't think there'll be any class. Maybe you
should ...

Owen begins picking up his texts. Doalty goes to him.

Doalty Is he long gone? – Manus.

Owen Half an hour.

Doalty Stupid bloody fool.

Owen I told him that.

Doalty Do they know he's gone?

Owen Who?

Doalty The army.

Owen Not yet.

Doalty They'll be after him like bloody beagles. Bloody, bloody fool, limping along the coast. They'll overtake him before night for Christ's sake.

Doalty returns to the window. Lancey enters – now the commanding officer.

Owen Any news? Any word?

Lancey moves into the centre of the room, looking around as he does.

Lancey I understood there was a class. Where are the others?

Owen There was to be a class but my father...

Lancey This will suffice. I will address them and it will be their responsibility to pass on what I have to say to every family in this section.

Lancey indicates to Owen to translate. Owen hesitates, trying to assess the change in Lancey's manner and attitude.

I'm in a hurry, O'Donnell.

Owen The captain has an announcement to make.

Lancey Lieutenant Yolland is missing. We are searching

for him. If we don't find him, or if we receive no information as to where he is to be found, I will pursue the following course of action. (*He indicates to Owen to translate.*)

Owen They are searching for George. If they don't find him –

Lancey Commencing twenty-four hours from now we will shoot all livestock in Ballybeg.

Owen stares at Lancey.

At once.

Owen Beginning this time tomorrow they'll kill every animal in Baile Beag – unless they're told where George is.

Lancey If that doesn't bear results, commencing forty-eight hours from now we will embark on a series of evictions and levelling of every abode in the following selected areas –

Owen You're not – !

Lancey Do your job. Translate.

Owen If they still haven't found him in two days' time they'll begin evicting and levelling every house starting with these townlands.

Lancey reads from his list.

Lancey Swinefort.

Owen Lis na Muc.

Lancey Burnfoot.

Owen Bun na hAbhann.

Lancey Dromduff.

Owen Druim Dubh.

Lancey Whiteplains.

Owen Machaire Ban.

Lancey Kings Head.

Owen Cnoc na Ri.

Lancey If by then the lieutenant hasn't been found, we will proceed until a complete clearance is made of this entire section.

Owen If Yolland hasn't been got by then, they will ravish the whole parish.

Lancey I trust they know exactly what they've got to do. (*Pointing to Bridget.*) I know you. I know where you live. (*Pointing to Sarah.*) Who are you? Name!

Sarah's mouth opens and shuts, opens and shuts. Her face becomes contorted.

What's your name?

Again Sarah tries frantically.

Owen Go on, Sarah. You can tell him.

But Sarah cannot. And she knows she cannot. She closes her mouth. Her head goes down.

Owen Her name is Sarah Johnny Sally.

Lancey Where does she live?

Owen Bun na hAbhann.

Lancey Where?

Owen Burnfoot.

Lancey I want to talk to your brother – is he here?

Owen Not at the moment.

Lancey Where is he?

Owen He's at a wake.

Lancey What wake?

Doalty, who has been looking out the window all through Lancey's announcements, now speaks – calmly, almost casually.

Doalty Tell him his whole camp's on fire.

Lancey What's your name? (*to Owen*) Who's that lout?

Owen Doalty Dan Doalty.

Lancey Where does he live?

Owen Tulach Alainn.

Lancey What do we call it?

Owen Fair Hill. He says your whole camp is on fire.

Lancey rushes to the window and looks out. Then he wheels on Doalty.

Lancey I'll remember you, Mr Doalty. (*to Owen*) You carry a big responsibility in all this. (*He goes off.*)

Bridget Mother of God, does he mean it, Owen?

Owen Yes, he does.

Bridget We'll have to hide the beasts somewhere – our Seamus'll know where. Maybe at the back of Lis na nGradh – or in the caves at the far end of the Tra Bhan. Come on, Doalty! Come on! Don't be standing about there!

Doalty does not move. Bridget runs to the door and stops suddenly. She sniffs the air. Panic.

The sweet smell! Smell it! It's the sweet smell! Jesus, it's the potato blight!

Doalty It's the army tents burning, Bridget.

Bridget Is it? Are you sure? Is that what it is? God, I thought we were destroyed altogether. Come on! Come on!

She runs off. Owen goes to Sarah who is preparing to leave.

Owen How are you? Are you all right?

Sarah nods: Yes.

Don't worry. It will come back to you again.

Sarah shakes her head.

It will. You're upset now. He frightened you. That's all's wrong.

Again Sarah shakes her head, slowly, emphatically, and smiles at Owen. Then she leaves.
Owen busies himself gathering his belongings. Doalty leaves the window and goes to him.

Doalty He'll do it, too.

Owen Unless Yolland's found.

Doalty Hah!

Owen Then he'll certainly do it.

Doalty When my grandfather was a boy they did the same thing. (*simply, altogether without irony*) And after all the trouble you went to, mapping the place and thinking up new names for it.

Owen busies himself.
Pause.

(*almost dreamily.*) I've damned little to defend but he'll

83

not put me out without a fight. And there'll be others who think the same as me.

Owen That's a matter for you.

Doalty If we'd all stick together. If we knew how to defend ourselves.

Owen Against a trained army.

Doalty The Donnelly twins know how.

Owen If they could be found.

Doalty If they could be found. (*He goes to the door.*) Give me a shout after you've finished with Lancey. I might know something then. (*He leaves.*)

Owen picks up the Name-Book. He looks at it momentarily, then puts it on top of the pile he is carrying. It falls to the floor. He stoops to pick it up – hesitates – leaves it. He goes upstairs.

As Owen ascends, Hugh and Jimmy Jack enter. Both wet and drunk. Jimmy is very unsteady. He is trotting behind Hugh, trying to break in on Hugh's declamation.

Hugh is equally drunk but more experienced in drunkenness: there is a portion of his mind which retains its clarity.

Hugh There I was, appropriately dispositioned to proffer my condolences to the bereaved mother...

Jimmy Hugh –

Hugh ... and about to enter the *domus lugubris* – Maire Chatach?

Jimmy The wake house.

Hugh Indeed – when I experience a plucking at my elbow: Mister George Alexander, Justice of the Peace. 'My tidings are infelicitious,' said he – Bridget? Too slow. Doalty?

Jimmy *Infelix* – unhappy.

Hugh Unhappy indeed. 'Master Bartley Timlin has been appointed to the new national school.'
  'Timlin? Who is Timlin?'
  'A schoolmaster from Cork. And he will be a major asset to the community: he is also a very skilled bacon-curer'!

Jimmy Hugh –

Hugh Ha-ha-ha-ha-ha! The Cork bacon-curer! *Barbarus hic ego sum quia non intelligor ulli* – James?

Jimmy Ovid.

Hugh *Procede*.

Jimmy 'I am a barbarian in this place because I am not understood by anyone.'

Hugh Indeed – (*Shouts.*) Manus! Tea!
I will compose a satire on Master Bartley Timlin, schoolmaster and bacon-curer. But it will be too easy, won't it? (*Shouts.*) Strong tea! Black!

The only way Jimmy can get Hugh's attention is by standing in front of him and holding his arms.

Jimmy Will you listen to me, Hugh!

Hugh James. (*Shouts.*) And a slice of soda bread.

Jimmy I'm going to get married.

Hugh Well!

Jimmy At Christmas.

Hugh Splendid.

Jimmy To Athene.

Hugh Who?

Jimmy Pallas Athene.

Hugh *Glaukopis Athene?*

Jimmy Flashing-eyed, Hugh, flashing-eyed! (*He attempts the gesture he has made before: standing to attention, the momentary spasm, the salute, the face raised in pained ecstasy – but the body does not respond efficiently this time. The gesture is grotesque.*)

Hugh The lady has assented?

Jimmy She asked *me* – I assented.

Hugh Ah. When was this?

Jimmy Last night.

Hugh What does her mother say?

Jimmy Metis from Hellespont? Decent people – good stock.

Hugh And her father?

Jimmy I'm meeting Zeus tomorrow. Hugh, will you be my best man?

Hugh Honoured, James; profoundly honoured.

Jimmy You know what I'm looking for, Hugh, don't you? I mean to say – you know – I – I – I joke like the rest of them – you know? – (*Again he attempts the pathetic routine but abandons it instantly.*) You know yourself, Hugh – don't you? – you know all that. But what I'm really looking for, Hugh – what I really want – companionship, Hugh – at my time of life, companionship, company, someone to talk to. Away up in Beann na Gaoithe – you've no idea how lonely it is. Companionship – correct, Hugh? Correct?

Hugh Correct.

Jimmy And I always liked her, Hugh. Correct?

Hugh Correct, James.

Jimmy Someone to talk to.

Hugh Indeed.

Jimmy That's all, Hugh. The whole story. You know it all now, Hugh. You know it all.

As Jimmy says those last lines he is crying, shaking his head, trying to keep his balance, and holding a finger up to his lips in absurd gestures of secrecy and intimacy. Now he staggers away, tries to sit on a stool, misses it, slides to the floor, his feet in front of him, his back against the broken cart. Almost at once he is asleep.

Hugh watches all of this. Then he produces his flask and is about to pour a drink when he sees the Name-Book on the floor. He picks it up and leafs through it, pronouncing the strange names as he does. Just as he begins, Owen emerges and descends with two bowls of tea.

Hugh Ballybeg. Burnfoot. Kings Head. Whiteplains. Fair Hill. Dunboy. Green Bank.

Owen snatches the book from Hugh.

Owen I'll take that. (*in apology*) It's only a catalogue of names.

Hugh I know what it is.

Owen A mistake – my mistake – nothing to do with us. I hope that's (*tea*) strong enough. (*He throws the book on the table and crosses over to Jimmy.*) Jimmy. Wake up, Jimmy. Wake up, man.

Jimmy What – what-what?

Owen Here. Drink this. Then go on away home. There

may be trouble. Do you hear me, Jimmy? There may be trouble.

Hugh (*indicating Name-Book*) We must learn those new names.

Owen (*searching around*) Did you see a sack lying about?

Hugh We must learn where we live. We must learn to make them our own. We must make them our new home.

Owen finds a sack and throws it across his shoulders.

Owen I know where I live.

Hugh James thinks he knows, too. I look at James and three thoughts occur to me: A – that it is not the literal past, the 'facts' of history, that shape us, but images of the past embodied in language. James has ceased to make that discrimination.

Owen Don't lecture me, Father.

Hugh B – we must never cease renewing those images; because once we do, we fossilise. Is there no soda bread?

Owen And C, Father – one single, unalterable 'fact': if Yolland is not found, we are all going to be evicted. Lancey has issued the order.

Hugh Ah. *Edictum imperatoris.*

Owen You should change out of those wet clothes. I've got to go. I've got to see Doalty Dan Doalty.

Hugh What about?

Owen I'll be back soon.

As Owen exits:

Hugh Take care, Owen. To remember everything is a form of madness. (*He looks around the room, carefully,* *as if he were about to leave it for ever. Then he looks at Jimmy, asleep again.*) The road to Sligo. A spring morning. 1798. Going into battle. Do you remember, James? Two young gallants with pikes across their shoulders and the *Aeneid* in their pockets. Everything seemed to find definition that spring – a congruence, a miraculous matching of hope and past and present and possibility. Striding across the fresh, green land. The rhythms of perception heightened. The whole enterprise of consciousness accelerated. We were gods that morning, James; and I had recently married *my* goddess, Caitlin Dubh Nic Reactainn, may she rest in peace. And to leave her and my infant son in his cradle – that was heroic, too. By God, sir, we were magnificent. We marched as far as – where was it? – Glenties! All of twenty-three miles in one day. And it was there, in Phelan's pub, that we got homesick for Athens, just like Ulysses. The *desiderium nostrorum* – the need for our own. Our *pietas*, James, was for older, quieter things. And that was the longest twenty-three miles back I ever made. (*Toasts Jimmy.*) My friend, confusion is not an ignoble condition.

Maire enters.

Maire I'm back again. I set out for somewhere but I couldn't remember where. So I came back here.

Hugh Yes, I will teach you English, Maire Chatach.

Maire Will you, Master? I must learn it. I need to learn it.

Hugh Indeed you may well be my only pupil. (*He goes towards the steps and begins to ascend.*)

Maire When can we start?

Hugh Not today. Tomorrow, perhaps. After the funeral. We'll begin tomorrow. (*Ascending.*) But don't expect too much. I will provide you with the available words and the available grammar. But will that help you to interpret between privacies? I have no idea. But it's all we have. I have no idea at all. (*He is now at the top.*)

Maire Master, what does the English word 'always' mean?

Hugh *Semper – per omnia saecula.* The Greeks called it '*aei*'. It's not a word I'd start with. It's a silly word, girl. (*He sits.*)

Jimmy is awake. He gets to his feet.
  Maire sees the Name-Book, picks it up, and sits with it on her knee.

Maire When he comes back, this is where he'll come to. He told me this is where he was happiest.

Jimmy sits beside Maire.

Jimmy Do you know the Greek word *endogamein*? It means to marry within the tribe. And the word *exogamein* means to marry outside the tribe. And you don't cross those borders casually – both sides get very angry. Now, the problem is this: Is Athene sufficiently mortal or am I sufficiently godlike for the marriage to be acceptable to her people and to my people? You think about that.

Hugh *Urbs antiqua fuit* – there was an ancient city which, 'tis said, Juno loved above all the lands. And it was the goddess's aim and cherished hope that here should be the capital of all nations – should the fates perchance allow that. Yet in truth she discovered that a race was springing from Trojan blood to overthrow some day these Tyrian towers – a people *late regem belloque superbum* – kings of broad realms and proud in war who would come forth for Lybia's downfall – such was – such was the course – such was the course ordained – ordained by fate ... What the hell's wrong with me? Sure I know it backways, I'll begin again. *Urbs antiqua fuit* – there was an ancient city which, 'tis said, Juno loved above all the lands.

Begin to bring down the lights.

And it was the goddess's aim and cherished hope that here should be the capital of all nations – should the fates perchance allow that. Yet in truth she discovered that a race was springing from Trojan blood to overthrow some day these Tyrian towers – a people kings of broad realms and proud in war who would come forth for Lybia's downfall . . .

Black

APPENDIX

Greek and Latin Used in the Text

page 2 Τὸν δ' ἠμείβετ' ἔπειτα θεὰ γλαυκῶπις Ἀθήνη
(Homer, *Odyssey*, XIII, 420)
Lit: 'But the grey-eyed goddess Athene then replied to him'
ἀλλὰ ἕκηλος ἧσται ἐν Ἀτρείδαο δόμοις
(Homer, *Odyssey*, XIII, 423–4)
Lit: '... but he sits at ease in the halls of the Sons of Athens ...'

page 4 Ὣς ἄρα μιν φαμένη ῥάβδῳἐπεμάσσατ' Ἀθήνη
(Homer, *Odyssey*, XIII, 429)
Lit: 'As she spoke Athene touched him with her wand'
κνύξωσεν δέ οἱ ὄσσε (Homer, *Odyssey*, XIII, 433)
Lit: 'She dimmed his eyes'

page 5 Γλαυκῶπις Ἀθηνη
Lit: flashing-eyed Athene

page 6 Αὐτὰρ ὁ ἐκ λιμένος προσέβη
(Homer, *Odyssey*, XIV, 1)
Lit: 'But he went forth from the harbour ...'

page 7 ὅ οἱ βιότοιο μάλιστα (Homer, *Odyssey*, XIV, 3–4)
Lit: '... he cared very much for his substance ...'

page 8 Esne fatigata?: Are you tired?
Sum fatigatissima: I am very tired
Bene! Optime!: Good! Excellent!

page 11 Ignari, stulti, rustici!: Ignoramuses, fools, peasants
Responde – responde!: Answer – answer!

page 12 θέος a god
θέα a goddess

page 14 Nigra fere et presso pinguis sub vomere terra

          Land that is black and rich beneath the pressure
              of the plough
          cui putre: crumbly soil
page 21 adsum: I am present
          sobrietate perfecta: with complete sobriety
          sobrius: sober
          ave: hail
page 22 caerimonia nominationis: ceremony of naming
          βαπτίζειν: to dip or immerse
          baptisterium: a cold bath, swimming-pool
page 23 Gratias tibi ago: I thank you
          studia: studies
          perambulare: to walk through
          verecundus: shame-faced, modest
page 24 conjugo: I join together
          acquiesco, acquiescere: to rest, to find comfort in
          procede: proceed
page 25 Silentium!: Silence!
          diverto, divertere: to turn away
page 26 ἄπληστος πίθος: unfillable cask
          Jacobe, quid agis?: James, how are you?
page 31 Festinate!: Hurry!
page 32 Gaudeo vos hic adesse: Welcome
page 33 Nonne Latine loquitur?: Does he not speak
            Latin?
page 35 opus honestum: an honourable task
page 50 Quantumvis cursum longum fessumque moratur
          Sol, sacro tandem carmine vesper adest
          No matter how long the sun delays on his long
            weary course
          At length evening comes with its sacred song
          expeditio: an expedition
page 65 Tu es centurio in exercitu Britannico: You are a
            centurion in the British Army
          Et es in castris quae sunt in agro: And you are in
            the camp in the field

page 87 domus lugubris: house of mourning
infelix: unlucky, unhappy
Barbarus hic ego sum quia non intelligor ulli:
I am a barbarian here because I am not
understood by anyone
page 91 edictum imperatoris: the decree of the
commander
page 92 desiderium nostrorum: longing/need for our
things/people
pietas: piety
Semper – per omnia saecula: Always – for all
time
page 93 *ἀεί* always
ἐνδογαμεῖν to marry within the tribe
ἐξογαμεῖν to marry outside the tribe
Urbs antiqua fuit: There was an ancient city
late regem belloque superbum: kings of broad
realms and proud in war